AWARD WINNING AUTHOR

KAY LYONS
STOCKHAM

SECRET SANTA

SECRET SANTA by Kay Lyons Stockham

Electronic and print editions published by

Kindred Spirits Publishing House, October 2014.

Copyright © 2014 Kay Lyons Stockham

Cover Art © @ olgaaltunina, ©Subbotina

Cover Design © Kindred Spirits Publishing

ISBN-13: 978-1502719867

ISBN-10: 150271986X

Copyright 2014 by Kay Lyons Stockham.

For all of those who
BELIEVE

CHAPTER ONE

"Mayday, mayday. Anchorage Tower, this is McGarretty, do you copy?"

The Cessna's engine sputtered again, earning a mutter from Ty as he piloted the small plane through the cloud bank obscuring his view of the Brooks Mountain Range. He was surrounded by a world of white—white clouds, white snow, unable to see anything other than the rapidly fading daylight.

Static crackled in his headphones but the tower didn't respond. He battled the wind gusts blowing in from the Arctic, his gut a tight, hard knot. Midair was not where he wanted to be in weather like this. "Mayday, mayday, Anchorage Tower, do you copy?"

Despite triple checking the forecast in order to take advantage of the hour and thirty-five minutes of Alaskan daylight, a snowstorm had appeared out of nowhere, blown in from the Chukchi Sea. Now he found himself off course somewhere along the rugged mountain range, struggling to keep the only thing between him and the ground in the air. "Come on, *Nessie*. Thatta-girl."

A sharp gust forced *Nessie* into another stomach-churning nosedive.

Blood pumped hard and fast in his ears, the loud, rushing pulses strangely in tune with the wind tossing him about like a trailer in a twister.

Ty's insides locked into a stopper knot when the clouds parted, revealing a bowl-shaped mountain he recognized from his maps. He was so far off course no one would look for him here.

Nessie lifted and dropped, the air sucked from beneath her wings. The bounce jarred Ty's teeth.

The Cessna's engine sputtered once more, pushed to the limits as it fought the force of the elements outside. In the end, the sudden quiet that came after the plane's last choking wheeze told Ty all he needed to know. "Anchorage Tower, this is Ty McGarretty. Can you hear me?"

His stomach lurched as the plane began to lose altitude. "Mayday, mayday! I'm going down. Repeat: I'm going down." He relayed his coordinates, not knowing if those systems were operating correctly or if anyone heard him.

Come on, God, is this really the way it ends? "Can *any*body hear me?"

Static filled his ears as adrenaline flooded his body.

Down, down, down. The raging winds of the snowstorm kept the plane aloft and prolonged the inevitable, rocking it from side to side like a sadistic tilt- a-whirl run by a drunken carnie.

His shoulders and arms ached as he fought to keep the nose up, every nut and bolt rattling with the force of the descent. Prayers spilled from his lips and he apologized to God for slacking when it came to church attendance. He'd do better. Take the kids. *If I make it home.*

Images flashed through his mind in rapid succession as he stared at the wall of white outside the window. And even though no one could hear him on the radio, there were things he needed to say. "Gramps, I love you, old man. Make Logan watch some cartoons and get his nose out of a book. And Abbie—don't let her date until she's twenty-five and has a black belt. I'm sorry about this, Gramps. Just do the best you can with the kids."

A sudden burst of static crackled from the radio and a woman's voice filled his headset.

"McGarretty? I can hear you."

Ty latched onto the sound of the woman's voice. "Get a message to my grandfather. George McGarretty in Anchorage."

"I-I will. I heard you."

Treetops. That's all he could make out in the blowing white mess below him, a quick glimpse when the plane swung hard to the left. Big, pointy treetops of massive pines that would rip *Nessie* apart before she ever hit the ground. Not a pleasant way to— Was that a strip of white?

"Keep your nose up. I'll be there as soon as I can," the woman said. "I'll find you."

His eyes burned from the strain of trying to make out the image but he zeroed in on the possibility, determination battling reality. "What's your name?"

Yeah, that was definitely white. One small, impossibly short strip of snow-covered valley floor. He'd made it to the interior of the mountain. *God, please. I can't leave them. Gramps won't last much longer.*

"Holly. My name is Holly."

The plane hit the snow, the bone-jarring impact followed by an ear-splitting noise as the wheels sank into the depths of the soft surface and were ripped off. The Cessna's belly acted like a big sled, plowing through the valley and gaining speed.

Ty bounced along, strapped in his seat unable to see anything but a rush of white until *Nessie* smacked into trees.

Pain hit, stole his breath, the sharp, copper taste of blood and bitter cold air choking him.

Time slowed as his body pitched forward and then back, jerking and yanking him like a rag doll.

Dazed, he felt the Cessna list to one side before she settled with a jarring *thunk* of metal.

A whooshing rush rolled over him, too strong to fight. Shivering from the cold, he felt himself slipping away…

***

"What are you doing, Holly? Stay where you are. Holly? Answer me."

Holly ignored the voice on the other end of the portable radio and frantically raced to dress. Every second counted and considering she had to harness the dogs, she didn't have time to respond to Devon's order.

"Don't even think about leaving your cave. The storm is getting worse. I'll handle it," Devon continued.

She stepped on the towel at the base of the hot springs pool where she had been relaxing when Ty McGarretty's distress call had sounded, twisting her feet in the cotton to dry them before snagging socks and hopping around on one foot while she yanked the wool over the other.

"Holly, I know you can hear me. Do not leave the cave!"

"I don't take orders from you, Dev." Racing across the cave floor she grabbed the layers she had stripped off earlier, hands shaking as she forced herself to take the time to put them on even though the pilot's words echoed in her head.

The last thing she needed was to head out into the cold unprotected and wind up freezing as a result. Underwear, tank top, thermals, two pairs of fleece-lined leggings, a sweatshirt, her snowsuit.

She dropped into the recliner behind her to stab both legs into the pants of the suit at the same time, battling the voice in her head that warned against hoping she might find Ty McGarretty alive.

But she couldn't just sit there and listen, wait, and do nothing.

"Holly, please. Stay put."

"I can't do that, Dev." One boot was near the recliner, the other... Where was the other? "Seriously? Come on, come on. Where are you?"

A man's life was at stake. If the pilot was alive, his odds were diminishing with every second that passed. And he had a family. Kids. Young kids from the sound of it. And only a grandfather to watch over them?

She dropped to her knees and looked beneath the coffee table. "You've got to stay more organized, Holl."

She'd been so ready to escape to her cave she'd stripped as she'd entered the innermost cavern, tossing her clothes with every step.

But there it was. From her position on all fours she spied the boot by the bed. How did it get all the way over there?

She scrambled up, carrying the first boot in her hand.

"Holly, for the love of-- Answer me!"

Holly groaned as she positioned the boots to shove her feet inside, reaching blindly with her free hand to find the radio she'd dropped onto the bed after responding to Ty McGarretty. "I'm closer. I'm going, Devon."

"I'm putting together a team. You are to stay put."

"I'm not going to argue with you. I'm going. Holly, out."

She heard his growl of frustration loud and clear despite the static.

"Holly, will you let me do my jo—"

She twisted the knob on the radio, muting Devon's voice. As head of security for their off-the-grid compound Devon took his job very seriously, as he should. But sometimes... What was it with men and their egos? Seriously.

Boots tied, she raced across the cave floor and up into the outer chamber where her sled dogs waited, away from the heat of the pool but protected from the harshness of the weather. "No rest for you guys," she called, ignoring their sharp barks as she gathered up harnesses and rigging and set about preparing them.

Thankfully her team was well-behaved and the dogs knew the drill, pacing around her and barking as they waited their turn to be harnessed, eager to see where they were going and no doubt picking up on her emotions about the need to rush.

Finally she stepped on the runners and forced herself to inhale a steadying breath. "Easy," she commanded, the order for the team to go slow until they left the cave.

She hated the time it took for her to fasten the gate over the opening of her sanctuary but it had to be done to keep unwanted animals from getting inside.

But then... "Hike! Moxie, *hike!*"

The command to 'mush' had Moxie and all the other dogs digging in and they were on their way, racing down the mountain.

The trail to the valley was winding but well-known by the dogs. Once they made it to the valley floor, she let them run full-out toward the far end, careful to stick to the edge of the forest so that she didn't inadvertently pass the wreckage.

The plane wasn't on fire. She tried to take comfort in that as she searched the darkness for signs of the crash, praying feverishly that the pilot wasn't dead. Holly knew they were getting close when the sled sailed past a wheel.

Then she saw it. The small plane was nose-first into the trees at the rim of the valley. Her heart stopped in her chest.

How could anyone survive that?

You of all people should believe in miracles. Show some faith.

She set the snow hook, even going so far as to tie the snug line at the back of the sled to the closest tree to keep the dogs from getting spooked and taking off on her. If they did, neither she nor the pilot stood a chance.

Holly scrambled around the tail of the plane and attempted to prepare herself for what she might find inside.

Please don't be dead.

***

"Hey! Hello? Mr. McGarretty? *McGarretty*, can you hear me? Come on, open your eyes. Open your eyes!"

Ty hated the annoying voice pulling him from a warm, deep sleep.

"*Ty McGarretty, open your eyes.*"

He heard a groan, vaguely recognizing it as his own. Waking up a bit more, he realized he wasn't as warm as he thought. Where was that draft coming from?

"Oh, thank God. That's it," the woman continued. "No, don't close your eyes!"

Ty turned his head away from the voice deafening his right ear, a wave of nausea washing over him. Ah, man. What had old man Arnold fed him before take off, a plate of food poisoning?

"*Listen to me.* Are you listening? I can't get you out of here on my own and we can't wait for help or we'll freeze to death. Wake up before we both turn into icicles."

The woman's desperate tone, her fear, cracked through the heavy weight holding him submersed.

Ty jerked his head up, groaning again because of the pain skittering through his brain as a result. Where was he? "What happened?" His eyes burned and were coated with something sticky.

"Here. Let me."

The woman wiped a cloth over his face.

"Ow," he said with a flinch, blinded by the piercing pain jabbing into his brain because of the bright light pointed in his direction.

"Sorry. I'll move it."

It took some time for the pain to fade and his gaze to adjust but the sharp smell of fuel cleared more of the cobwebs from his brain.

Fuel. He rolled his head on the seat and stared at the face hovering in front of his. "We have to get out of here."

"That's right. But you have to help me."

Help her. Was she hurt?

He narrowed his gaze on the woman speaking to him and the shadow she cast became clearer. Mouth. Nose. Wide eyes. Beautiful, beautiful face. A dark stain on the white scarf hanging from her neck. "You're hurt."

"What? No. No, I'm fine. I used it to wipe the blood off *your* face. I'm okay. You're the one who's hurt."

"Good." He didn't like it when others were hurt, especially women.

"Keep those eyes open, McGarretty."

The cold seeped into his skin and made him shiver. "You sound like...my CO."

"Ahhh, military, huh?"

"Yeah—or, I was." Why was everything so confusing?

He shifted in the seat and grimaced. His muscles were cramping, locking up from the cold. What were they doing out here?

"You can tell me all about it as soon as we get you out of here."

Ty nodded his understanding, bits and pieces coming back to him in chaotic flashes. Flying. The snowstorm. Radioing for help.

He'd crashed?

"Can you breathe okay? Anything broken?"

"No. I don't think so." He lifted his hand to his aching head.

She gently turned his face toward hers.

"Oh, that cut is still bleeding like crazy. Here, maybe this will help."

She took off her scarf and wrapped it around his head several times, fitting his knit cap over it to hold it in place once she was done.

"That will have to do for now. The wind's blowing so hard I'm afraid we might flip. Can you move your legs? Knees and toes and everything in between? Ribs okay?"

Her questions flew at him faster than he could process them with his scrambled brain but he got the gist. He shifted again, moving one foot into the small area where she stood hunched over him. So far so good.

But then he tried to move his left foot and couldn't.

"What's wrong?"

Something held him trapped. Ahhh, poor *Nessie*. "Help me up."

His rescuer unbuckled the straps holding him in place and retreated in the cramped confines so that she could wrap her arms around him from behind. Ty tried to exit the seat but his left foot was pinned. A few gentle yanks didn't budge it but every pull sent pain streaking up his leg.

"Stop," she ordered. "Are you hurting yourself?"

His throbbing brain bounced off the inside of his skull and his arms shook with the effort it took to hold himself upright on one foot while trying to free the other in the unstable plane. "Get out of here. I'm coming."

Her hands tightened against his stomach. "I'm not leaving you. Let me help."

The woman moved so that she balanced over the pilot seat, the headrest shoved into her stomach, her hands extended to help free his trapped leg.

Ty twisted, pulled, groaned at the pain, and finally managed to get his foot unstuck from beneath the collapsed control panel.

"Is it broken?" she asked, back on her feet.

He put his weight on his foot. Another surge of nausea bubbled into his throat when pain ripped through him, but dazed as he was, Ty managed a thankful prayer. At least his foot was still attached. "We'll find out later."

He straightened as much as he could inside the damaged hull of the Cessna, sliding an arm around the woman's shoulders at her urging.

"Don't pass out on me," she ordered, raising her voice to be heard over the howling wind. "I can't carry you and with that bump on your head you have to stay awake. Get used to me asking you if you're awake. Got it?"

"Yeah. I hear you." Even as he said the words his lashes felt weighted, his eyes burning from the sting of blood. "I can't see."

"Just hold onto me—and this. Don't drop it."

She pressed the flashlight into the hand of the arm he had wrapped around her shoulders, and he gripped them both like lifelines.

The woman helped him to a hole ripped out of *Nessie's* side. She eased him to the floor and Ty clutched the flashlight while she exited the plane.

"Come on. Lean on me."

The wind blew them into *Nessie's* body once they made it out but the plane also acted as a barrier and kept them upright.

The pain forced him to dig deep into a place he didn't know existed to keep moving when all he wanted to do was close his eyes and sleep. Every step blasted black and red spots in front of his eyes and left him gulping for air and sweating.

It wasn't until they reached *Nessie's* tail that he was able to hear impatient barking and blinked his eyes clear enough to see the long outline of the sled team that awaited them. "Sled dogs?"

"Hey, don't knock it! They're a lot safer than flying in this!" Her quick response was followed by a husky laugh that was carried away by the wind.

"Where are the others?" The storm was growing stronger—or else he was growing weaker. And colder.

"It's just us," the woman said, panting from the effort of keeping them both upright.

Just her? She'd braved this weather alone?

The frigid temperature penetrated his clothing, shards of ice biting into his face as they left the protection of the Cessna and stumbled forward.

"Sit there," she ordered, helping him down onto the basket at the front of the sled.

Ty groaned his relief, grateful to be off his foot. His teeth chattered, and he could feel the moisture on his skin freezing, his entire body jerking and twitching uncontrollably.

So. *Cold.*

"Ty. That's your name, right?"

It was hard to speak when his teeth chattered enough to cut off his tongue. "Yeah."

His rescuer dropped blankets over him. "We've got a lot of ground to cover and we have to do it fast. I know it's going to be hard to stay awake once you get warm but you *have* to fight it. *Don't go to sleep.*"

"Okay." He couldn't hear himself say the word and he doubted she heard it, either.

Think of Gramps. Beth's kids. You can't leave them alone in this crazy world.

"Stay with me, McGarretty. I don't want to get to where we're going only to find you dead."

Beneath the blanket he forced his lashes up, his eyes open, able to see the swirling snow thanks to the lantern his rescuer had fastened above him. It was like being inside a snow globe.

"Holly to base. He's alive! I have him," she yelled. "I'm bringing him in."

Ty heard a man's voice but couldn't make out the words.

"No, it's too far! Just be ready for us! Holly, out. Moxie! Moxie, *hike!*"

***

Holly stared out at the thickening snow and reminded herself she had no choice. The snowstorm had become blizzard-like in its intensity, the temperature and conditions getting progressively worse.

Forget the rules. This was life and death. Not only Ty McGarretty's but potentially her life and those of the dogs. An exception could be made under such extreme conditions.

Outsiders were banned from the compound. No exceptions.

Until now.

She knew the time was coming when her father—and the rest of the compound and their organization—expected her to fill his position as organization leader, protector, village elder and mentor. This was her first step in that direction.

In a situation like this, life took precedence over the risk. Ty needed more medical attention than she could capably dispense. The only thing *to* do was take him home to the compound.

She shifted her weight on the runners, dreading the confrontation she faced. Everyone inside their off-the-grid home would know she had broken their most sacred rule. Right now Devon was no doubt sounding the alarm, placing the village on lockdown so there was as little movement as possible.

She would answer for her actions. Be held accountable. Not to Devon—she refused to answer to him—but to her father and the Elder Council.

But why should the pilot suffer needlessly when the compound's doctor was a sled-ride away? What rule was worth risking a man's life?

And when Ty McGarretty is better? Alert?

Then... Then they would deal with him but at least he would *be* alive.

Having reached the end of the valley, she urged the dogs into the forest, up the path that wound through the mountains.

The dogs were eager, and despite the blinding snow and wind they made good time, though it seemed to take hours because she was so aware of the pilot's injuries.

Moxie led the team into the final turn approaching the village and Holly leaned into the curve, her eyes bleary and body heavy from the long day and the fading adrenaline rush of the rescue.

Devon's demand for her to meet him on a trail away from the compound so as to allow Devon to take the pilot on to the next closest village was too dangerous. Not only for Ty McGarretty but Devon and the guards responsible for transporting the pilot over mountains in the middle of this as well.

The temperature had dropped by several more degrees and the bitter wind gusts were so bone-chilling she wished for another layer.

The dogs pulled them higher, deeper into the concealing forest, midway up the mountain.

She glanced down, the lanterns attached to the sled allowing her to see the top of Ty's knit hat despite the mound of blankets she had placed over him. His face was covered, and the whiteout conditions forming around them kept her from having to take the false trails and add to their time.

Twenty minutes later Holly approached the compound's east entry and found Devon waiting along with some of his men outside of the guardhouse.

She could see the anger in Devon's expression and her heart picked up speed. "Whoa," she called to the dogs, commanding them to stop.

She could feel multiple sets of eyes on her, peering out from within the compound's buildings and the many small cottages dotting the woods around them. The trees protected them from the worst of the wind but the air around them was filled with the popping and cracking sounds of branches breaking beneath the weight of the snow and ice.

"Take him to the infirmary," she said to the guards. "Is Jamie waiting?" she asked Devon.

"Yes."

The word was growled, low, and bordering on a hiss. Holly lifted her chin and turned to the guard stepping onto the sled's runners. "I'll be there soon to take the dogs home."

"Yes, ma'am."

The guard got the sled moving, and despite the cold and the snow chilling her to the bone, Holly waited, determined to stand toe to toe with Devon rather than show weakness.

Finally he bit out a word under his breath and opened the door of the building. *Best to just get it over with,* she mused.

"What have you done?" Devon asked once they had stepped inside.

Devon's office was by the exit and Holly walked toward it without hesitation, hearing the exterior door opening again to admit several of Devon's men.

"I've saved a man's life. And probably yours," she said, moving directly to the old-fashioned heating stove. "What's the latest weather report?"

Devon shut his office door. "A blizzard advisory has been issued."

So she was right. Spend as much time in the forest as she did and a person learned to read certain things. Not that Devon apparently appreciated the fact. "The pilot has a concussion, and his foot may be broken."

Devon closed the distance remaining between them. She was tall at five-feet-eight but Devon was taller and she had to tilt her head back to maintain eye contact.

"You should have let us take care of him."

"I was closer," she countered. "He could have frozen to death before you got to him."

"You are our future. You should not be risking yourself. And bringing him here?"

"He is in no condition to travel. How could letting him remain exposed to the weather and untreated until you showed up, and *then* hauling him over mountains, be anything but cruel?"

Staring up into her friend's handsome face she saw the way Devon's brown eyes had turned molten-gold with his upset.

She waited impatiently, refusing to give in and voice regret she didn't feel, simply because she knew it's what he wanted. *Not gonna happen.* "Why are you really upset, Devon? Because I disobeyed the rules... or you?"

"Don't change the subject. I'm merely trying to do my job."

"And I'm trying to do mine—which is set an example as the future leader of this community."

"And you think you did that tonight?"

"Yes! I showed compassion. I proved that I would not allow someone to suffer needlessly when I could do something about it."

"Even though by bringing him here, you've risked us all because of your inability to follow the rules?"

Holly fisted her gloved hands and forced her shoulders to lower from her ears. The scent of wood smoke and baked goods teased her senses and made her stomach growl, her body aching for heat and food and the comfort of her bed. But Devon had to be handled first. "He's barely conscious and saw nothing of the trails. You couldn't see more than a few feet in front of you out there. It will be fine."

Devon didn't appear convinced despite her reassurance.

"Holly, your father left the security and safety of this village and everyone in it to me. That includes you. When I told you to stay put—"

"I do not take orders from you." She stated it softly but there was no denying the strength of her tone, the purpose. She would not bow down. If Devon liked her? Wanted her? If in time they had a future together? He had to accept her for who she was.

He ran a hand over his head, yanking off his cap in visible frustration.

"You had no idea what you were getting yourself involved in. You had no idea what he was carrying, if the plane might explode. If he was dangerous!"

"It didn't. He wasn't. And when someone's life is at stake, are those really the things to ask first?"

"You could have been injured getting him out of the wreckage. What would you have done then?"

Now he had her. Because with that question he revealed a wealth of emotion on his face and seeing it made her feel guilty that she'd worried him. Devon had been her friend since childhood and if anyone had a clue of the pressures she faced, it was him. "I would have dealt with the problem. The same way you would have dealt with it."

"I would have had others there to help me."

And she had been entirely alone. She thought of the way the plane had rocked in the wind, unsteady, ready to flip. "Look, Dev, I can't say it won't happen again," she said as a concession, "but I'll remember that next time."

A rough huff of a laugh rumbled out of his chest and he shook his head at her.

"I mean it. I hear what you're saying but you can't argue about things that didn't happen. I understand your concern but I am here now, see?"

"Concer—" Devon broke off, the word muffled by the gloved hand he ran over his mouth.

Obviously irritated, he yanked the gloves off and tossed them onto his desk, scattering papers in the process.

"Holly, what I feel for you is more than *concern*. When are you going to see that?"

She saw it now. She heard it in his voice, felt it in the tension he carried. And she cared for him, too. Growing up they had been friends, good friends. But things had changed since she had taken on more responsibility from her father and Devon rose amongst the ranks of the guards.

Maybe, if things were different and she didn't feel like Devon wanted to control her, she might feel more for him. But she had so much ahead of her, so much to learn, that she couldn't add the pressure of dealing with Devon to it. "I was fine."

"I don't like it when you're out there alone. Especially when I think you're safe and then you go sledding into a blizzard."

"It was just a little snow," she said, managing the words with a smile.

Devon settled his hips against the edge of his desk and stared at her.

"Invite me to come with you next time. You know I would welcome the invitation— and keep you safe."

Devon had offered to accompany her before and while she *had* considered it a time or two, she had also found herself making excuses and putting him off. Of all the men in her village Devon was... the best. The most handsome, the most commanding, the most interesting to her. But still... "It's my private place," she said, recognizing disappointment in Devon's gaze before he disguised it. "One I'm not ready to share yet." Not with Devon, not with anyone.

Devon stood and moved to sit in his desk chair. The position of authority?

"Anna is worried. Go home and put her mind to rest."

"I will—after I check in at the infirmary," she said, taking the opportunity to leave.

"*Holly.*"

She barely managed to restrain a laugh at his flummoxed expression and moved toward the door. "Goodbye, Dev."

"Keep it up and your father will return early, just because you've gotten on his bad side," Devon called after her, his tone grumbling.

Truth be told, if she continued breaking the compound's rules, being on her father's bad side would be the least of her worries.

CHAPTER TWO

Ty opened one eye and debated the effort required to open the second. His head throbbed, his brain pulsing with every *thud-thud-thud* of his heart.

He shut out the bright white lights of the room and tried to remember how he'd gone from... Where had he come from?

Assorted memories appeared in slow bits. The snowstorm. The crash. A woman. Dogs? Things got fuzzy again after that.

He forced his lashes up a second time, blinked against the pinpricks of harsh light and groaned. Yeah, definitely not worth the effort.

"Hey. Noooo, don't go back to sleep. Come on, wake up. You're starting to worry us."

Something cool and moist touched his forehead, a welcome relief to the throbbing.

"Head still hurt?" a woman whispered.

"Sledgehammer," he muttered, ungluing his tongue from the roof of his mouth. Her voice sounded familiar but he couldn't remember her name. It was her, though. His brave rescuer. He would never forget her face. "Who are you again?"

"You don't remember?"

He pictured her hovering over him in the wreckage, holding him upright as they made their way to a sled. "I'd call you Angel."

Low, throaty laughter filled his ears and brought a weak smile to his lips. He might not remember her name but he remembered that laugh.

"Yeah, well, after everything you've been through, I'm not surprised you have a few missing pieces to the puzzle. My name is Holly."

Holly. The voice on the radio. Yeah, he remembered that. "How long was I out?"

"Two days."

There were machines in the room, an IV in his left arm and a cuff around his upper right arm ready to take his blood pressure.

A heart monitor beeped somewhere behind him on the right. "Where am I?"

"The infirmary."

An infirmary? "Where?"

"It's, um— I brought you here on my sled."

How off course was he? Most of the villages or outposts had first-aid kits, maybe a nurse or EMT in town if they were lucky. But none of them had the equipment he was currently attached to in one form or another.

"I'm happy to see you're finally awake," she said, smiling down at him from beside the bed. "We were worried."

"I've been out for days?"

"Yeah. We got here just in time. The snowstorm turned into a blizzard right as we arrived. We're back to a severe snowstorm advisory that's sticking around. Things are really nasty out there."

He shifted in the hospital bed and bit back a groan. There wasn't a single bone or muscle in his body that didn't feel like it had been shredded and glued back together by a kindergartener.

"Easy."

His body felt weighted, his mouth dry. "I'm fine. Just sore. Thank you," he added, the words gruff. "You shouldn't have put yourself in danger to get me but I'm thankful you did."

"You're welcome. I'm glad I was able to help."

He was, too. But now he needed to get home. Fast.

He grabbed the cuff on his arm to remove it, but she grasped his hand in hers and stopped him.

"What do you think you're doing?"

"Leaving."

"Uh, no. You just woke up."

"I have to get back to Anchorage."

"You're not ready to go anywhere, Mr. McGarretty. Not yet."

His head swirled so badly he fell back against the bed. She was right about that. One wrong move and he'd be kissing the floor.

Holly squeezed the hand she held and he got the brief impression of strength and softness.

"You're dizzy, aren't you? See? Stay put."

It wasn't like he had much of a choice. He had to. For now, anyway. "What day is it?"

"It's Wednesday morning, almost lunch time, not that you can tell from looking outside. You slept through the last day with sunlight in this part of Alaska. We're officially twenty-four hours of darkness. And in case you missed what I said earlier? It hasn't stopped snowing since we arrived. No one is going anywhere in this weather."

Not what he needed to hear. "My grandfather has the kids. He can handle a few hours with them but not days. He's not up to that." Gramps was seventy and not in peak physical condition.

"You have children?"

He rubbed his hand back and forth across his forehead hoping to ease the throbbing. "My niece and nephew. I have custody. My sister's deceased."

He still couldn't wrap his head around that fact, either. There was something greatly wrong with a world that took a mother from her young children. The kids would have been so much better off with Beth. What he and Gramps knew about raising kids could fit inside a thimble.

Holly's expression softened at his words. "I see. Well, I'm sure they will be very happy to see you when you get home but you're not up for the trip just yet, trust me. The good news is that you're awake, and your foot isn't broken but severely bruised and sprained. Jamie— the doctor—said if you take it easy you'll be good to go in no time. Maybe by the time the weather front passes through, we can get you out of here."

He shifted in the hospital bed again, only then realizing his injured foot was propped up by several stacked pillows. He spied the button to raise himself up and pressed it.

"Oh, I'm not sure you should—"

"I want to sit up." Splitting headache or not, a man had no pride lying flat on his back in a hospital bed. He needed to shake off the grogginess and come up with a plan.

Holly waited patiently by the bed while it slowly raised his head and shoulders. Once he was where he wanted to be, she placed an extra pillow behind him.

Man, she smelled good. Like crisp winter air and vanilla and something spicy and sweet, like cinnamon.

"Better?"

"Yes," he said, wondering how anyone could be as physically tough as Holly had to be as a musher, and yet so beautiful. Her long blond hair hung loose over her shoulders and when she turned away to cross the room he saw that she wore a thick sweater over leggings and shaggy, fur-like boots that were more stylish and feminine than he remembered seeing in Alaska.

But while her beauty appealed, it was her kindness and strength he admired most. How many women would brave the Alaska bush in the middle of a blizzard for someone who, technically, shouldn't be alive?

Thank you, he said to The Man Upstairs.

"I feel partially to blame for your condition," Holly said. "Not the crash, of course, but because you were exposed to the cold for so long in the cockpit until I was able to reach you."

"You made it. That's all that matters." Holly handed him a cup of water and he drank greedily, the cold easing a little more of the pain. "I'm grateful you found me at all. I wouldn't be here without you. I'm not sure how I'll ever repay you."

Holly could have been hurt coming after him like she had and grateful or not that she'd saved him, he didn't like the awareness that she'd risked herself.

A brief hint of a smile curled her lips up at the corners, softening the worried lines on her face.

"No payment required. So, ah, are you hungry? You've been stirring quite a bit so I had Alicia bring some soup and fresh rolls. Feel up to eating?"

He inhaled and got another whiff of her perfume along with something that made his mouth water. "Yeah, now that you mention it. Smells good."

Holly retrieved a tray and set it on the adjustable table across his bed, lifting the cover and arranging things just so.

When she finished he grabbed the spoon and dug in, knowing he looked a bit sluggish because he felt that way.

She watched him at first. Busied herself by opening a container of apple juice, but then turned and paced the room.

"Something wrong?" he asked. The soup was more broth than anything but there were little bits of meat and vegetables mixed in. Now that he was sitting upright and sipping on the hot soup, the ache in his head was lessening to a dull pounding.

"No. No, not at all. I'm just so relieved you're awake and feeling better. You shouldn't overdo it, though. In fact, I should go and let you eat. The doctor will be in soon to check you and—"

"Wait." He felt like something that had been run over twice and left to die, but no man in his right mind would send a beautiful woman like Holly away. "Stay a few more minutes. Please."

Holly tucked her hair behind one ear, the move sweet because it was so innocent. She looked like a complicated mix of sweet and soft.

"Ty, you need to rest, and I have to get back to work."

"What do you do when you're not hanging out in the infirmary?" he asked, hoping the question would get her to stick around and give him a few more answers.

He tore off the top of the roll and dipped it into the broth. Man, that was good. He was so hungry he could eat a moose, and with every bite he woke up a bit more. As long as he didn't move his head too much or too fast, he was okay.

"I work for my father. I'm a bookkeeper and secretary, plant waterer. Whatever the day calls for."

He finished off the broth, wondering if he could get another bowl. "Where am I again?"

She gathered up her coat and a tote bag of a purse. "In the bush," she said simply. "Rest. As soon as you're up to it, I'll sled you out to get a supply flight, okay? For now all you need to do is eat, sleep and get well."

He settled down into his pillows, his body heavy and tired despite his determination not to be. "I have to call Gramps. Let him know I made it." He carefully turned his head and searched the room for a phone but when he didn't see one he glanced back at Holly in time to catch a flicker of something in her expression. The softness he'd seen seconds ago disappeared, replaced by a carefully blanked expression and lift of her chin.

"I'm afraid we're old school. The infirmary doctor takes a holistic approach to healing. Quiet. Peace. Good food. No phones or outside distractions in the room like televisions or radios. So you truly rest," she added, nodding like not having a television was a *good* thing. "But don't worry, I found your contact information in your wallet and I was able to send a message to the email address you had listed. I said you're okay, and will be home as soon as possible."

Ty sighed his relief. Gramps loved tinkering with the computer and checked his email account pretty often during the day. No way would he miss the news. "Thanks. I appreciate it."

"You're welcome. So relax, okay? Now, I should—"

"I still want to talk to him myself, though. Do you have a cell phone I can use? A satellite phone?"

Holly shifted her weight from foot to foot, her coat and bag in front of her. "No. But you rest, and I'll see what I can do. We're remote, and getting word out can be tricky, especially when we're experiencing a snowstorm like the one outside. But I'll try to set something up as soon as I can, okay?"

It would have to be. He didn't like the thought of not talking to Gramps right away but so long as his grandfather knew the crash wasn't fatal... "Yeah, sounds good. Thanks."

"You're welcome."

He lifted what was left of the roll. "The food helped. I'll be on my feet in no time."

"That's good to hear," a man said, drawing their attention to the doorway.

The guy was tall, six-two or -three, and dressed in gray, black and white winter camo topped by a black thermal cap, a Glock at his side and black snow boots.

Wait— Where was he again? A military base?

Ty zeroed in on the gun. A lot of Alaska's residents were armed given the fact they lived in bear-prone and isolated areas where animals—both human and the four-legged variety—were unpredictable. But this guy made Ty believe the man wasn't dressed for hunting. His choice of weapon for one. And the beard?

Neither were military. The gun because it wasn't standard issue, and the beard because they weren't allowed due to facial hair interfering with getting a good gas mask seal.

"Ty, this is Devon Sage. Devon is our village sheriff," Holly said, standing between his hospital bed and the man blocking the exit.

Ah, so that explained the uniform. And the Glock most police favored.

The man dipped his head in greeting, his expression dark. "Nice to hear you're making a quick recovery. Holly, I stopped by your office but you weren't there," Devon said, acting as though it was a regular occurrence. "Have you finished visiting the patient?"

Ty got the impression Devon aimed to make a point—that of Holly's presence being a charitable one and nothing else.

"As a matter of fact, I have," she said to Devon. "Ty, get some rest, okay? I'll be back to see you tomorrow."

"I look forward to it. Thanks for being here when I woke up." He held out his hand and waited until she retraced her steps and placed her warm palm in his.

Giving him one last smile, Holly walked to the door where the sheriff waited, a dark expression on his face.

As they left the room Ty pressed the button and lowered himself down to a more comfortable position, fatigue stealing over him.

There was nothing he could do in the shape he was in except sleep and heal and be ready to face the mess he'd find at the house once he made it back to Anchorage.

He closed his eyes and let his mind drift, picturing the Brooks Mountain Range in his head. He had studied every inch of those maps, memorizing towns and outposts, the terrain.

Why didn't he remember a village big enough to have an infirmary or a sheriff in this area?

Better still, why he didn't remember seeing a village at all?

Devon didn't speak to Holly as they walked down the hall and out the doors of the infirmary but the moment they stepped outside, he took hold of her arm and tugged her into a two-seat alcove along the entry that shielded them from the wind and blowing snow.

"What are you doing?" he demanded.

"What do you mean?" She stared up at Devon, still more than a bit unnerved by the glorious green of Ty's eyes.

"Don't give me that. You don't need to order him food or sit at his bedside. And you need to stop calling the infirmary to check on him because people are talking enough as it is."

Because she had broken the rules and brought Ty McGarretty into the compound. And shocking though it was, people were taking sides. The risk of her actions versus the humanity of them. "So I'm just supposed to dump him here and not care?"

"Care? Sure. But you seem to be a little too caring given the circumstances."

"Jealous?" she quipped, not expecting an answer.

"Maybe I am."

Devon growled the words, making her feel guilty for her snarkiness.

Jealous? Really? She wasn't sure what to make of that. A part of her was secretly flattered by Devon's ongoing attention but it didn't change facts. She was too busy for any entanglements right now. "Look, Devon, I know you're wanting to take our friendship to another level but I've told you the time isn't right for me. Things are too busy and chaotic. For *both* of us."

"It doesn't have to be."

"But it is."

Devon's gaze turned dark brown. "You're too busy—yet you can visit him for hours every day?"

Okay, so that wasn't the best excuse but still... "He's alone and injured. And he's *here* because of me."

"That answer doesn't help your case, Holly."

"What case? What do you mean?"

"It means you're already in enough trouble with the Elder Council because you brought him here. Heed my warnings and don't see him anymore."

Or what? Maybe it was childish of her but, come on, seriously? He expected to tell her who she could and couldn't see? Could and couldn't save? For real? "I said I would visit Ty tomorrow and I will."

Devon glowered at her but she didn't back down. If it was her, or any other member of their community in the same situation, she wouldn't want to be alone. Wouldn't want to be left behind. Where was the compassion in that? The humanity they worked so hard to preserve? "Don't look at me like that. I know you don't like this situation, but what's the saying? The one about how if you save someone you're responsible for them? That's how I feel. Let me handle this, Dev. You don't need to be involved."

Oh, she really touched a nerve with that. Devon's expression turned positively dark.

"You're playing with fire. I don't know why you insisted on doing this, but you know it's going to end badly. Think about it, Holly. What happened last time?"

Yeah, she got it. Last time their location was discovered, word got out and the village had to move, becoming the example used ever since for *what not to do*. "He'll be out of here as soon as he's on his feet."

"And then what? The word you're avoiding is curious. He knows about us now. And if he tells someone there will be people talking, nosing around."

"You're being paranoid. It won't go that far."

"The world is a worse place now than it was then, Holly. The last time outsiders were allowed in our people were *devastated* by the fallout and had to go deeper into hiding."

"I'm well aware of our history." But she refused to doubt her decision to save Ty. It was the best decision to be made at the time. Period. Now they would make the next best decision to suit the circumstances.

"Then let him heal but keep your distance. Jamie can handle him. It's best for everyone if you stay away. The less he knows about you, the better."

Maybe that was true. Maybe it wasn't. But if she backed down she knew Devon would take it as a sign that she was bowing to his will. She couldn't help but think the real reason Devon didn't want her seeing Ty was because of the jealousy he'd just admitted to. Which meant giving in took on a whole other meaning...

"Holly, everyone in this compound is watching you."

"Good. I hope so because I did what was right. They're wrong if they think otherwise."

"*Holly.*"

"*What*?" she said, losing her patience. "Dev, don't you ever get tired of it? Of always being watched and used as an *example*? Don't you ever wonder what it would be like to have a normal life?"

"Now you're questioning your *life*?"

The way Devon stared at her she felt like a bug under a microscope. "*No.* No, I'm not. I know exactly what is expected of me but I'm saying there is more out there than just us. We watch the world from afar but when it falls into our lap we can't simply ignore it. What kind of people are we if we do that?"

"Careful ones. *This* is our life, Holly. This *is* normal," he said, his voice low and full of meaning. "What's gotten into you?"

Into her? Really? "I'm horrified by the thought that anyone here—*any*one— would ever think risking someone's life is more important than shouldering a little inconvenience until the patient heals enough to be transported *safely* out."

Devon stared down at her for a long time, his hands braced on his hips. The wind blew, swirling around them in the little alcove, her hair catching in the gloss on her lips.

Before she could move Devon reached out and brushed the hair from her mouth, tenderly stroking her cheek with his gloved fingers.

The touch was gentle, sweet, the look in his eyes one of blatant frustration but care and concern, too. It would make things so much easier if their personalities meshed better than they did. Many people would be happy to see her and Devon together. But until she knew for sure... "I know who I am, and I know what I have to do in order to be able to look myself in the mirror," she said softly. "And I'm not sorry."

She sidestepped Devon and crossed the narrow porch to the ramp.

The snow fell thick and steady and obscured many of the cottages from view as she crossed the street to return to work, but the few cottages visible were picturesque and endearing, just like the people, her friends, inside them.

She couldn't deny Devon's words of warning. Having Ty McGarretty in the compound was taking a huge risk.

Maybe if she dug into Ty's background? If she could set their fears at ease? She knew enough about Ty's life from his comments about having custody of his sister's children and his grandfather to know learning more *could* be…endearing. And hopefully enough to buy Ty time to heal.

The wind picked up, rushing around her and blinding Holly momentarily.

She turned her head to protect her eyes and found Devon behind her, his long strides quickly closing the distance between them.

Sometimes, at her loneliest, she wished her heart would sputter and pound for him the way she had read about in books. Every night she prayed to find the right man for her, one who would want a wife at his side, who would fully support her when she took her rightful place as head of the organization.

Devon understood the pressures she was under, understood their life of secrecy. It would be so easy to fall into a relationship with him, to seek comfort from him from the long, sometimes trying days. But it wouldn't be fair to Devon, not when that voice inside her whispered for her to *Wait*.

"I understand why you went after him. I don't agree with it, but I understand it.

And the last couple days... He's a curiosity to you," Devon said, falling into step beside her. "But we both know he can be nothing more."

"Then no one has anything to worry about, do they?" she countered, meaning every word.

"Do you think it's going to be any easier on McGarretty if he gets to know you and then you disappear once he's back in Anchorage? I can tell you the answer."

The words struck deep and Holly's stride faltered for a brief moment at the horrific thought before she charged full speed ahead. Once Ty was able to travel he would be gone, unable to return. "I'll keep my visits brief. Having told him I will return, not going would only draw more questions from him. It could potentially raise his curiosity and create more problems."

Dev lifted his hand and ran it over his jaw and the carefully trimmed beard he wore year-round. She knew Devon pondered her words when he didn't argue. "I have to get back."

She turned to go into her building when Devon caught her arm in a gentle grip.

"The reason I was looking for you is because the elders have scheduled an emergency meeting with your father upon his return."

The news rocked her. A knot formed in her stomach despite her absolute conviction that she had done the right thing and would rescue Ty again if need be. "They're coming here? *Now*? But it's—"

"You can't expect them to do nothing."

"I understand that. I knew there would be consequences but—" She broke off, her thoughts bounding from fear to anger to sadness because her parents were going to be so upset. Embarrassed.

What would the Elder Council decide? How do you punish the leader's *daughter*? A slap on the wrist? Or something more extreme to set an example for the future leader of what would not be tolerated by the people she had to protect?

"Holly," Devon said, drawing her attention. "What are you going to do if they decide to send you north?"

It took some doing but she managed to put on a brave face. "I'll go. I'll accept whatever they decide."

"Holly, be *sorry*," Devon ordered. "Be contrite and apologetic. This isn't just about McGarretty. It's about our life here, our purpose. Our very existence."

"You think I don't know that? I do. *That* is why I rescued him." She backed away from Devon, toward the steps into her building, holding his gaze. "Dev, I know what you're saying and why. But I *won't* apologize."

Holly turned and jogged up the steps, hurried inside. She ignored the stares she felt as she crossed the interior but once inside her office she closed her door and leaned against it, giving herself thirty brief seconds to freak out before she smoothed her hair, took a deep breath and forcibly calmed her nerves.

The Elder Council obviously insisted on doling out a punishment for risking the compound's safety. And because she was her father's daughter she would deal with whatever they decided.

But if she thought it was cold here...

CHAPTER THREE

Holly kept herself busy the rest of the afternoon, stopping long enough to attend the evening church service where she caused a stir with her appearance. She bolted from the church the instant service was over, pretending to not hear the several who called her name. Returning to her office, she worked late into the evening before walking home and going straight to bed.

The next day she was tired from tossing and turning but she went to work anyway, ignoring the sharp stabs of guilt she felt as the clock ticked by the hours. She'd promised to visit Ty today and she planned on keeping that promise. But she'd be lying if she said her conversation with Devon about the Elder Council meeting and the congregation's reaction last night didn't make her wary. The elders might excuse a life and death situation but her *continued* fraternization with an outsider? Visiting Ty would only place her in a worse light.

Her conflicting feelings of guilt both in regard to Ty and to the people in her care distracted her from the spreadsheets and columns and numbers she was supposed to be tallying for her father.

While her father was away she had to make sure business stayed on track and things were progressing as planned, but her mind kept wandering and she found the facts and details of shipment dates, product and delivery times, blurring before her eyes.

She picked up the phone on her desk, her fingers hovering over the numbers that would connect her to the infirmary's main desk.

She hadn't lied when she told Ty his room didn't have a phone but the nurses' station did and she wanted so badly to call again, to check on Ty *again*.

Instead she forced herself to replace the handset and maintain a modicum of composure where Ty was concerned. Not for his sake or hers but for her parents. She didn't want them bombarded with gossip and considering the Elder Council was waiting with bated breath... "Get to work, Holl. Focus."

Priorities, right? She knew her priorities.

So maybe that was her defense when the time came? Because after the crash Ty was most definitely in her care?

Really? That's what you're going with?

She tossed the pen aside and buried her face in her hands. *God, please help me explain this....*

Because now that Ty was there—how was she going to get rid of him?

***

Three hours later Holly smoothed her hands over her sweater and tried to calm the flutter inside her that came as a result of going to see Ty again.

Her response was ridiculous. He was just a man, an outsider. Right? Her nerves were from the awareness of the consequences and nothing more.

It was late. Too late for her to be bothering Ty but when she had turned off the lights in her office and left, she couldn't force herself to break her promise to visit him. She'd given her word and she would keep it.

As she crossed the village street she glanced at the guardhouse that held Devon's office as well as her father's on the second floor.

Devon was either inside at his desk, in his quarters or out on patrol, checking one of the many security systems around the perimeter of the compound. Winter storms like the one they were experiencing meant downed limbs and trees, iced lines that snapped and had to be repaired. Devon had his hands full with those problems and finalizing the routes.

And hopefully he's too busy to notice your whereabouts?

She entered the infirmary and shivered thanks to the temperature difference. Jamie was nowhere to be seen but Alicia was at the nurse's desk, bent over a chart. The woman looked up as she heard Holly's approach.

"He's been asking for you."

Holly smiled weakly, aware of the woman's gaze raking over her, noting every detail. "Lots of work to do."

"That time of year," Alicia replied. "I'm hoping to get my tree put up tonight. My son is so excited. Do you have yours up?"

"No. No, Anna and I are waiting for my parents to return."

"Of course."

Holly kept walking and reached Ty's room. She gently rapped on the door before letting herself in. If he was asleep she would leave.

Please be asleep.

"Hey, beautiful. There you are. I thought you'd ditched me."

She blinked at the endearment, wondering why hearing it from him gave her such a pleasant thrill. She was a sensible woman, one who knew not to have her head turned by flattery. "I said I'd be back."

"I know, but when it started getting late I figured you'd taken something Barney said to heart."

"Barney?" she repeated, confused but glad to see Ty not only sitting up but looking rested, with color in his cheeks, and the pain so apparent behind his eyes yesterday, gone.

"Yeah. Barney Fife? From the old TV show?"

"Oooooh," she said, catching on and smiling because of the comparison. Devon would *hate* being compared to the bumbling sheriff's deputy considering he was so well-trained. "Don't mind him. Devon is just protective."

"And why is that?" Ty asked.

Stepped right into that one, didn't you? "Uhhm..."

"You know, I've had lots of time to think today and I was wondering... You two a couple?"

That's what he'd thought about all day? "No."

"But he'd like to be," Ty said, his gaze unwavering.

"Is that a question or a statement?" she asked, shutting the door partially behind her in the hopes it would keep their conversation from carrying to the nurse's desk—and yet open so she didn't garner any more.

"A simple yes or no will do."

She took in Ty's handsome face and dark hair. The deep, pine green eyes. *You must have made quite a sight in your service uniform.* "No. We're not. Devon and I are good friends, though."

"Bet that busts his ego."

She wasn't about to comment on that statement. Even if she knew it was true.

Why, oh, why couldn't she feel more for
Devon? "What about you?" she asked,
turning the tables in an attempt to make
conversation. "Aren't bush pilots like sailors,
with a girl at every outpost?"

Ty grinned. "Some, maybe. But there's
only one special girl for me."

"Oh?" she asked before she could stop
herself. Why she asked she didn't know.
Especially since she felt a niggle of unease
while she waited for his response.

"Yeah. She's a beauty. She has the biggest,
prettiest green eyes you've ever seen,
corkscrew black curls. And every time I
tickle her...she pees on me."

Holly burst out laughing at the image.
He'd really had her going there for a minute.
"Please tell me you're talking about a pet—
or your niece?"

He winked at her. "You catch on quick.
My niece, Abbie."

Since the tension had lightened after his
comment, she decided to stick to general,
less-intrusive subjects. "Have you had
dinner?"

"Yeah. I waited for you but when you
didn't show up my stomach got the best of
me."

"Well, considering you have nearly two days of eating to make up for I'm not surprised. But I did bring you something—dessert from home."

His gaze dropped to the bag in her hand. "I hope you brought enough to join me."

She had. But was it wise to stay? *Like you don't know the answer to that question?* "Actually, I should probably get going."

Ty pushed himself higher in the bed. "No way. I've been resting all day hoping you'd show. You can't run away yet."

"I'm not running away." The defense sounded weak even to her.

"Then stay. Just for a while?"

When a handsome, seemingly kind man with gorgeous eyes asked a woman to stay, how could she refuse? "Just for dessert."

Minutes later the chocolate-filled croissants were spread out on the adjustable hospital table. Holly sat at the foot of Ty's bed with her ankles crossed in front of her, Ty's injured foot propped on several pillows a few inches away. "So tell me what all Doc said," she ordered. "How's that knot on your head?"

"Wouldn't you rather talk about something else?

"We can—after you tell me." She softened the order with a smile. She needed to know what Jamie had told Ty so that she was ready to sled Ty out as soon as he was able to travel.

If she were smart she would allow Devon to handle the transfer because she really couldn't afford the time away from her desk—or more trouble. But since she had set the wheels in motion she felt it was a job only she should complete.

"My head is fine. I slept most of yesterday and today, so the headache is gone. And according to the doc I'm still a little too wobbly for crutches, but I should be okay to spend some more time on them by tomorrow."

"That's great. I'm sure your family misses you as much as you miss them. You must be anxious to get out of here and back to them."

"I am. But if there's time I'd like to buy you lunch or dinner. To say thank you for rescuing me."

"Oh. Uh... Didn't you just say you had to stay off your foot? I doubt you should be out there in the snow." She scrambled for an out. An excuse. Something. For a man who had been unconscious and unresponsive for nearly forty-eight hours Ty seemed to be recovering quickly.

How many prayers did you pray for just that?

Countless. But what were they going to do when Ty was up and about and he looked outside the window?

"What are crutches for?" he countered with a bold smile.

"That doesn't mean you should be wandering around and taking chances. You might slip and fall."

"It's a chance I'll take. I'd like to see where I landed."

"Oh, I can assure you there's nothing much to look at. It's just a village, like any other."

She said the words casually but felt Ty's stare lingering on her face. Did she have chocolate on her mouth? Her chin? Stuck to her front teeth?

She raised her napkin and shielded her mouth from his view while she did a quick check with her tongue. She didn't *feel* anything.

"No village is just a village, just like no city is just a city. Every one of them is different in some way. That's why I like exploring them."

So did she. And, okay, she'd give him that reasoning but still. "I suppose we do have our own uniqueness but there's really not much to see, especially with it snowing the way it is."

Ty tilted his head to one side. "Something going on you're not wanting to tell me?"

Holly grabbed her bottle of water and took a swift drink to keep from having to answer verbally, shaking her head. She wasn't good at hedging or redirecting the conversation, and for the first time she realized maybe she *was* in over her head when it came to dealing with Ty. What could she say to convince him to stay there and...sleep?

"What's the name of your town again?"

She nearly spewed water. Swallowing, waving a hand to excuse her rudeness, she coughed and coughed when it went down the wrong way. "Oh, sorry. And you wouldn't have heard of it. There's just a small group of us. We're not a town."

"Your village, then. What's it like living out here?"

A lifetime of warnings about sharing too much information barreled to the forefront of her mind.

Sometimes she wondered if all the secrets were overkill, that it was her father and the village elders taking matters to the extreme because of the *devastation* of the past. But as Devon had reminded her, how could they not be cautious? To protect themselves, secrets were required.

Best you never forget that, daughter-mine. Our way of life is sacred and meant to be protected, not displayed for the masses or ridiculed by non-believers. The outsiders have no idea what the world would be like without us.

Her father's teachings echoed in her head and reminded Holly of who she was. Why roots mattered more than anything. "There's not much to say. Home is home. Quiet. Peaceful. Like every other Alaskan village."

"Not all villages are so far removed from civilization, though. I don't even remember seeing you on the map."

"No, y-you wouldn't have. We're very private. One of my great-grandfathers settled here a long time ago and ever since then we've kept to ourselves." *Did you have to tell him that?*

"I see. So is me being here a problem?"

Something about the way he asked the question left her staring at him, wary and on edge. "Depends. Do we have any reason to worry?"

Ty's gaze softened to a molten green. Yeah, those eyes should be classified as lethal weapons.

Outsider, outsider, outsider.

And what about showing hospitality to strangers who just might be angels?

Holly took a long look at Ty and shook her head. She couldn't quite label Ty as an angel. He might be kind, might be considerate. But none of those things changed the fact he was an outsider.

The words played in her head, reminding her to be extra cautious. The truth was she couldn't take a deep enough breath because that something—that *zing*—that feeling she had every time she came near Ty thickened the air, the expression on Ty's face adding to the tension skirting along her skin, forging a connection unlike anything she'd ever felt before.

"No, sweetheart. You have no reason to fear me."

The endearment rocked her that time almost as badly as it had the first.

Habit, she told herself, like someone referring to a woman as honey or darling. It was sexist, too, but the soft, gravelly tone of his voice removed the need to correct him. "I'll bet you call every woman sweetheart."

The briefest hint of a smile flitted about Ty's lips, curling up the corners of his mouth.

"Only the pretty ones."

She added "flirt" to the mix of words to describe him, a dangerous combination. "I should, um, get going."

"Already? Come on, stay a little while longer. I haven't even had a chance to ask you about *Nessie*. Any chance I could get a look at her before I leave?"

"*Nessie*? Your plane?" she asked, connecting the pieces of information. "You named your plane?"

He made a show of looking insulted. "You name all those dogs you have?"

She laughed.

"If you can't take me, I understand. Maybe once the storm blows through I can come back and try to salvage some of her."

Holly squeezed the water bottle so hard it made a *crackling* sound in her hand.

Come back? Salvage her?

Ty obviously felt a bond with the small Cessna but the last thing she wanted was for him to return in a bigger plane or with other people.

Devon warned you. He wanted to keep something like this from happening. Had Devon gotten Ty out of the area right away, you wouldn't be scrambling to come up with an excuse now, would you?

She shifted on the bed, trying to buy some time. "Um, I hate to break it to you, but *Nessie* is a total loss. I passed her wheels on my way to find you that night, and the hull and cabin were completely destroyed. We left through a hole in the side. There's nothing to salvage. You don't remember?"

"Not really. Guess I shouldn't be surprised, though. It was a rough landing. I'd still like to see her. Take some pictures for the insurance company and myself."

"Oh, uh. Maybe. We'll see." Maybe she could use sledding Ty back to the wreck site to her advantage? It was easy to get turned around in the wilderness surrounding the patch of land where Ty had crash-landed. Maybe taking him to the plane and back out to one of the farthest villages to the northwest would disorient Ty enough to keep him from ever finding the area again?

Once Ty left, Devon and the others would take care of hiding the wreckage to keep it from drawing notice or becoming a marker for Ty to return to. If he was determined to see it, it would have to be soon. And the sooner he saw it, the sooner he left.

"Are you debating because Barney wouldn't like it?"

"Bar— *Devon* has nothing to do with it," she said, barely catching the slip and correcting herself. "Are you sure you even want to go back? I mean... after everything that happened? That crash was a close call."

"That it was. But unless you grabbed my stuff and I don't remember it, I've got supplies onboard I have to retrieve. They're presents for Gramps and the kids. Can't just leave them out there."

Ty's expression warned her that one way or another he was going to get to the crash site to retrieve those gifts. And maybe she could have denied him if he hadn't come up with a reason to go back that tugged at her heartstrings.

What if they're not gifts? If they're something else?

"I, uh, can't give you a firm answer right now," she said. "You're still recovering, and the snowstorm is pretty bad. The worst we've seen for a while."

Ty nodded his acceptance of her words but she could see he didn't like her indecision. "Okay, fine, I'll see what I can do—but no promises."

"Deal," he said, looking a wee bit relieved.

She picked at the flaky crust of the croissant, pondering the dilemma of how she might get Ty to the crash site and out of the village without him remembering the way.

Every pilot she knew was good at directions, like they had a built-in GPS in their head. Her father could wear a blindfold and still know where he was. Misleading Ty when he was fully cognizant wouldn't be easy. More likely it would be impossible.

And yet you're considering it, why? A change of subject was in order. "Have you always lived in Anchorage?

"No. I grew up in the Midwest then moved to New York as a teenager. It's a long story."

"I'd love to hear it."

"You want the story, you have to hand that over," he said, indicating what was left of her dessert. "You're playing with it, not eating it."

She did so without a fuss, glad Ty had not only regained consciousness but his appetite as well.

"Thanks. These are good."

"I'll be sure to tell the cook."

Ty finished off the treat in two bites while Holly waited patiently for him to continue. "Your story?" she prompted once he had swallowed the last of the croissant.

"Nothing exciting. My dad wasn't a wanna-be actor or anything like that. We—my dad, sister and I—moved to New York after my mother took off. Dad raised us with help from my grandma until she passed away. Gramps went a little wiry after that and decided he wanted to see the country. He wandered around for a while until he wound up here."

"And he liked Alaska so much he stayed?" She could totally imagine that. Alaska was beautiful. One of her favorite places on earth.

"Exactly."

"What did your father do for a living?" Maybe she was being nosy but she'd always found people's background interesting.

Where they came from, what they had done...

Ty's smile fell, his expression so heartrending she regretted asking the question.

"He was a first responder. He died on 9/11."

"*Oh*." The air left her lungs in a rush. Of all the responses Ty could have made, she wasn't expecting that.

He shifted uncomfortably in the bed and grimaced when he moved his foot.

She wasn't sure whether to drop the subject or press on. "Is that, um, how you wound up in the military?"

He nodded once. "When Dad was killed I signed up to serve. I was nineteen and full of fire."

"Where was your sister?" Because of his age, Ty wasn't exactly a child of 9/11 but close enough. She couldn't imagine going through so much, much less going through it virtually alone.

What kind of mother left her children?

"Beth was a college freshman. She was angry when I told her." A smile eased the shadow of pain on his face and lit up his expression. "She came up with this crazy plan to escape to Canada like people had in the 60s. Took me a good month to bring her around."

"She must have been ecstatic when you came home."

"She was."

Holly drew her knees to her chest, wondering how or if she dared to ask the next question that popped into her head. "What happened to her? If you don't mind me asking. How did you wind up with her children?"

Ty turned his attention to the napkin in his lap, grabbing it to wipe his mouth, his lashes lowered over his eyes.

"She moved to Anchorage to live with Gramps and get a new start. Mom leaving us did a number on Beth. Beth made some bad choices, had two kids with two losers who took off almost as soon as she told them she was pregnant."

"Oh, no." Her heart broke for the woman, unable to imagine the pain of being abandoned over and over again.

"Beth was driving home from work one night and hit a patch of ice. Flipped the car three times."

"I'm so sorry." Ty had suffered so many losses in his life. His story made her even happier that she had fought to save him.

"Me, too. Beth and I got close after our mother left, more friends than brother and sister. It was nice."

Holly blinked away the sting of tears. She wasn't an overly emotional person but someone would have to be made of stone to not sense Ty's heartbreak.

She glanced up and found Ty watching her, his green eyes staring into her like he wanted to see her soul. Her breath hitched in her chest, her pulse picking up speed.

All from a look?

Yeah, definitely best if Ty leaves as soon as possible.

"Something wrong?"

"What?" She blinked, realizing she had simply been sitting there staring at him. "No. No, just distracted."

"Because of Beth's story. Sorry, I shouldn't have said anything. It's not exactly uplifting conversation."

It was in a way. Because it showed who Ty really was. And just how far he would go to keep his little family together. "I asked and I'm glad you told me. But I really should get going."

He snagged her hand.

"Holly?"

"What?" The word emerged husky and low, revealing.

"Thank you. I've never met anyone like you. You are an amazing woman."

His hand slid up her arm and he used his hold to bring her just a wee bit closer to him.

"Thank you for rescuing me."

She stared into his eyes, her mind blasting her with silent orders to get out of there, away from him. But her body refused to move. Was he going to...?

Ty brushed her lips with his and her heart went wild, speeding out of control like it did when she and the dogs raced across the frozen tundra.

He hesitated then kissed her again. A sweet, heady caress that wasn't too bold or hard. Just...a kiss of hello and thanks and... interest? Seconds passed and her mind spun like a carousel.

Alicia cleared her throat, the sound loud and startling, before the other woman informed them that visiting hours were over.

Since when did they have established visiting hours?

"I guess that's your cue," Ty murmured, looking very much like a man saddened by the news.

She nodded and slowly straightened, the pit of her stomach a hard knot of unease that grew larger when she met Alicia's gaze.

***

"Holly, go home," Devon ordered, not looking up from his desk.

Holly stood on the threshold of Devon's office, still quivering from her mad dash from Ty's hospital room.

What had she done?

Seriously.

Why had she kissed him?

She wasn't sure who was more embarrassed, her—or Alicia. The poor woman had witnessed Holly's clumsy *hop* from atop Ty's bed and her frantic, can't-get-out-there-fast-enough departure.

And she knew—she *knew*—she had to face Devon now, get it over with, because it wasn't going to get any easier. "Dev—"

"I don't want to talk to you right now."

Oh... *Oh.* He already knew? Good grief, she'd just crossed the street from the infirmary! Had Alicia raced to the phone before Holly could make it out of the building?

"Don't look so surprised. Very little if anything goes on in this compound that I don't know about."

And there was her answer.

She tried to keep a flush of embarrassment out of her cheeks but it proved impossible when Devon sat back in his office chair and gave her a look like— Like the news had angered and hurt and devastated him all at the same time. Like *they* were more than they were. "Well... I don't owe you an apology or an explanation," she said, hearing the defensive tone in her voice and wincing.

Devon sat in his chair, his hand rubbing slowly back and forth across his chin. "Actually, you do when I am the one responsible for cleaning up your messes."

"You are not—"

"Alicia has been asked to keep her mouth shut. I don't know if it will work, but you'd better hope she does or else you can expect the Council will be in an even bigger uproar."

No, no, no. The Elder Council was the last thing she had been thinking about when she'd kissed Ty. But Devon was right. The gossip of her transgression would only add to the elders' anger and upset.

She blinked, wished she could undo the last ten minutes. Wished she could right the wrong she had unthinkingly and heartlessly committed.

A kiss wasn't worth the devastation and pain she would inflict on her family and friends. "Tell me what Alicia said."

Devon muttered something under his breath, the air rushing from his chest hard enough to rustle the papers in front of him.

"I called to check on the *patient* and discovered his tongue was down your throat."

"That's not— That's what Alicia *said*?"

"No. After I demanded to know what had her acting so strange she admitted you were there with him, kissing." Devon got up and paced across his office floor, his angry strides heavy and hard. "When your father finds out..."

"Why does he have to? Leave my father out of this."

Devon shot her a pained glance. "You know I can't do that. My loyalty is to your father. I tell him *every*thing that goes on while he's away, especially when it comes to outsiders. And you."

"Dev, it was a *kiss*. Why say anything when it won't happen again?"

Devon raked his fingers through his hair. "It wasn't just one break in protocol, Holly. You disobeyed orders and went to the crash, you brought him here, now this?"

"I assure you it will not happen again. What more do you want?"

"What more do I want? I want the only thing I've ever wanted—*you*. This," he said, his hand jerking toward the window or the room, she wasn't sure which.

The air left her lungs and didn't return. Blood pulsed in her ears, every gush drowning out her chaotic thoughts. How could life be so complicated? She wished she could give Devon the response he wanted to hear but....

"I have work to do. Go home, Holly."

Devon turned his back to her. She stared at the width of his shoulders and faltered, wanting to stay and talk the way they had been able to before their responsibilities and duties got in the way of their friendship. Wanting to go and hide away in her cave because she felt such a strange fascination about a man she didn't know, couldn't have, because of the rules and secrecy she lived and abided by.

She knew how busy Devon was. The last-minute decisions and preparations were being made for cargo transport and the horrible weather was wreaking havoc with everything. The last thing they needed was the complication of having Ty inside the compound. Of having what happened in the infirmary causing more tension and upset in their community.

She turned. Stopped. Remembered why she had come there in the first place. "Ty has possessions on the plane and wants to retrieve them. He's asked me to sled him back to the crash site so he can have one last look."

"*No*. If he's well enough to do that then he's capable of—"

"He's not ready yet," she said, hating Devon's expression and the glare of utter disbelief he shot at her.

"Tell him *no*. Better yet, I'll tell him. You stay away from him."

"The bags he wants contain presents for his family, Devon. His grandfather and niece and nephew. For *Christmas*."

Devon made a sound in his throat.

"If Ty has the items in his possession I can put him off about visiting the plane. He isn't up for that trip. Not yet."

"And yet he's well enough to kiss you?" Devon asked.

She hated his tone, so sardonic and hard. Tinged with jealousy?

In that moment she felt like a juggler who didn't know how to juggle, every ball tossed into the air on a direct course with the bulls-eye on her head. "I think it will raise more suspicion if we refuse Ty outright."

"Wasn't that your excuse for going to his room?" Devon asked, the words quietly spoken but thick with accusation.

"Once he's able to travel, I'll take him by the wreckage and out of the valley to get a supply flight from one of the villages. I can loop the paths enough to disorient him and we will never see him again. It will be over, Devon, and we can put this behind us."

When Devon didn't speak she walked to the window overlooking the center of the village and eased the curtain aside to look out, able to see shadows moving along the tree-lined paths, brief hints of light as doors were opened and closed.

Every window was covered as required, the village as dark as its surroundings to not draw notice from above and raise suspicions.

Sometimes she wondered if it was all worth it. If they were fighting a losing battle when it came to keeping their secret. If ultimately, it would all be for nothing because there would come a point when it wouldn't even matter anymore.

So many years. So many sacrifices. So much devotion to a world falling apart at the seams.

Sometimes it was hard to remember that their work was a calling and yet she had to stay faithful, especially since she would be taking the helm soon.

Her doubt made her wonder if she had what it took to lead her people, because she *didn't* agree with all of the rules and their traditional way of living.

When it became obvious that she wasn't going to leave until she had an answer, she heard Devon sigh.

"The items from the plane will be delivered to the infirmary tomorrow," Devon said, his voice devoid of emotion. "I'll see to it myself."

CHAPTER FOUR

Holly tried to stave off the headache behind her eyes with another mug of coffee heavily laced with cream.

Guilt was a horrible thing. It robbed a person of sleep, peace, and the ability to think straight. Then again, the aftereffects of kissing Ty did pretty much the same because her mind played the scene in his infirmary room over and over.

"Leaving. Outsider. Not happening," she whispered, hoping the reminder would finally sink in.

Her feet were weighted with lead as she approached her desk and stared at the mountain of paperwork she had to get through in the next week. Unable to force herself to take a seat and dig in, she moved to the window and raised the shade.

"Forget something?" Mari said as she stepped into Holly's office.

Her assistant flipped off the lights as expected.

Holly winced. How many ways could she screw up in such a short period of time? What else would go wrong? "Thanks."

"You okay?" Mari asked, dropping yet another binder of paper onto Holly's desk.

"Yeah, fine. Just tired."

"Wouldn't have anything to do with your gorgeous pilot, would it?" Mari asked.

"No. And he's not *my* pilot or anything else," Holly said firmly.

"Oh, come on," Mari said in a cajoling tone. "It's me."

Holly leaned her forehead against the cold windowpane and closed her eyes. "What have you heard?"

"Tall, dark, smoking hot—and you kissed him."

No. No, no, *no*. Alicia obviously hadn't kept her word. And then Holly remembered. "You're cousins. You and Alicia."

"Yup," Mari said, her tone way too cheerful. "But don't worry. Alicia only told me because she's worried about you and what would happen if others found out. I made her promise she would keep quiet."

But would she?

"Hey, are you okay? Really?" her assistant asked.

"Yes. I'm fine. Really." Holly turned and faced her desk, determined to drown herself in work and forget about the issues wreaking havoc with her emotions. "How long until all of this is computerized again?"

"Another year."

Holly sat down. Where would she be in a year? Maybe here. Maybe serving her punishment in the deep north. The Elder Council couldn't send her there forever, not when their future rested on her shoulders. But since her father wasn't looking to retire anytime soon... Would they make her stay until it was time for her to take over? To set an example?

The phone rang and Mari leaned across Holly's desk to answer it there.

"Hey, Alicia. What's up?"

Holly bit back a groan. What now? She locked gazes with Mari and watched as Mari's eyes widened, getting bigger and bigger as Alicia filled her in on whatever was going on.

"Okay. Yeah, thanks. I'll let her know. She's right here."

Holly leaned back in her chair, feeling the desperate urge to jump on her sled and take off to her cave. "What?"

"We have a problem," Mari said as she returned the handset to the base.

"So I gathered. What's wrong?"

"Darcy Phipps went into labor early. Jamie managed to stop it but she has to be monitored and off her feet. And since John Benning is in the second room..."

"They need Ty's room for Darcy." Had she really just wondered what else would go wrong?

Mari nodded. "Jamie would move Ty into John's room but the family is staying round the clock."

Because John was ninety-two and dying, his kidneys failing. The last thing his family needed to do was watch every word and action because of having Ty in the hospital bed next to John. "No, that won't work. John's family shouldn't have to deal with that on top of everything else."

The rooms were spacious enough to accommodate four hospital beds and equipped with privacy partitions that disappeared into the walls, ready to be used as needed. But it was too great a risk to have Ty in the same area. John's family was huge, with a lot of young children running around.

"Yeah, well, that's not all, I'm afraid. Your pilot knows about John and Darcy. Mr. McGarretty has decided to check himself out of the infirmary, like, as we speak."

"*What*?" Holly surged to her feet and grabbed her coat.

"What are you going to do?"

She raced for the door, donning her coat at the same time. "I have no idea."

***

Ty carefully pulled his freshly ripped jeans over his bruised and bandaged foot and balanced himself on the side of the bed long enough to tug the jeans over his hips.

He'd had enough of the infirmary. Of not having a television, a phone. Of the nurse—Alicia—giving him looks every time she walked by his door or into his room.

He'd kissed Holly. Big deal. He'd meant it as a thank you and... Okay, so maybe he wouldn't mind kissing her again. No one would blame him for that.

But apparently the kiss *was* a big deal the way Holly had taken off and disappeared last night. If anything spelled out the truth of the moment, it was her reaction.

Horror. Embarrassment. The stubborn tilt of her chin and lightning-flash speed of her bolting out the door.

It was just as well. He needed to get out of the infirmary, needed to get home.

Thankfully most villages usually had several guides willing to brave the cold for the right price. He just hoped it wasn't too high or else his lack of income and the hit to his savings would mean a lean Christmas the kids didn't deserve after losing their mother.

A knock sounded on the infirmary room door. Considering the doc or nurse typically walked right in, he paused in the act of zipping his freshly laundered jeans. "Come in."

"Hey, I heard you were—oh!"

He chuckled at Holly's reaction despite the kick in the gut he felt at seeing her again. "It's okay, I'm decent," he said, finishing off the button.

Holly glanced at him as though to make certain and then hovered nervously in the doorway, her face bright pink.

"I'm sorry, I didn't mean to barge in."

"I'm dressed. Mostly," he said, pulling on a shirt. "You here to talk about last night?"

"Uh… I suppose we should. Ty, that wasn't typical behavior for me. It shouldn't have happened."

"Life's a little complicated right now for me, too," he said, mourning the fact she regretted something that was quite special to him.

"Good. I mean, that's not good, but it's… no problem then, right? No harm done?"

"No harm done," he agreed.

She tried to smile but the attempt was weak at best. He narrowed his gaze on her, taking in her body language. Why was she so nervous? "You close shop early today?"

"Actually, Alicia called."

"So much for patient confidentiality."

"Please don't be angry. She's concerned. Ty, you can't just walk out of here. Not when you were unconscious a couple days ago."

"I'm fine now. No headache, I'm not dizzy, and there is no sense in taking up a bed when someone else needs it."

Holly moved toward him, and he found himself drawn in by her expression. By the softness in her pretty blue eyes.

"You're trying to be nice, but I get it. The infirmary is small and you know the situation with the rooms. Jamie says he can come up with another place for you to stay, though, even if it's in his office."

"No thanks. I'll find a place somewhere else."

"You're not fully recovered."

"The more I move around the better I feel," he told her. Truth was his foot ached and his muscles were sore from being tossed about in the crash, but he was tired of lying there staring at the walls.

All he could think about was getting to *Nessie.* If Holly didn't want to take him to the crash site, he'd need to hire an available guide, get his possessions, and figure out how he was going to get home. He couldn't do any of that from this room. "I've rested plenty. I won't overdo it."

She shoved both hands into her hair and pushed it off her face. "Where are you going to go? We don't have a motel, and the storm hasn't moved through. According to the weather it may not lift for *days,* and whether you will admit it or not, you aren't ready for the trip to the nearest village to get a flight out."

"You don't have supply flights here?" How did they survive?

"No. We don't have any flights."

Whoa. They were in the middle of nowhere. They had to get supplies from somewhere. "How is that possible?"

"We're ninety-nine percent self-sufficient, and whatever we need from the outside world, we get on our own through a variety of sources like my sled or Snow-trac or snowmobile."

"Wouldn't a supply drop be easier?"

"Maybe but— Ty, the village is very much off-the-grid. We've learned to rely on ourselves. You know, with the weather being as iffy as it is."

Okay, now that he could understand. The military had taught him to be a one-man warrior, self-reliant when he had to be, yet work as a team otherwise. Obviously her village had learned to depend on itself rather than be caught without supplies in the middle of a storm like the one raging outside. In this part of Alaska it simply made sense.

The fact that he was going to have to get to another village was definitely going to make getting back to Anchorage more difficult, but not impossible. *Gramps, I'm coming. Hang in there.*

Holly stalked over to stand in front of him, a frown pulling her eyebrows low. "I can't let you walk out of here with no destination in mind. I didn't pull you out of that wreckage just so you can be stubborn and freeze to death after you slip and fall into a snowdrift."

"What do you propose?" He waited for her response, watching the way her mouth trembled just slightly as she formed silent words.

Finally, after fisting her hands and wrinkling up her forehead like a wizened old woman, she said, "You can stay with me."

The words emerged in a rush of air that ran all the syllables together and made him wonder if he'd heard her correctly. "With you?"

That wasn't what she wanted at all. Her expression said that loud and clear. But Holly nodded, firm.

"Yes. You can stay with me at my parents' house. We have an extra room, and Anna is there. She can watch over you and help out until the snowstorm moves through."

"Anna?"

"My aunt."

If he had to stay, better to spend the time with Holly than at the infirmary. "Thanks for the hospitality. I appreciate it."

Ty donned his bloodstained but clean coat and grabbed his crutches, swinging himself toward Holly and stopping when she didn't move, like she couldn't believe she'd made the offer. He wasn't going to let her retract it, though. Staying with Holly could prove to be interesting. "Let's go home."

Checking himself out of the infirmary was surprisingly easy. Seeing as how it was a small facility, all he had to do was sign off on a sheet stating he was leaving against doctor's orders and that was that. According to Holly and the nurse, the bill would be sent to him later.

Ty followed the visibly tense Holly down the hall, every swing of the crutches giving his sore muscles a workout. Lying in a hospital bed for days hadn't helped his stiffness.

Outside, Holly's sled and a small team of three dogs waited at the bottom of the ramp. He stopped at the sight.

"Don't argue," she said from behind him.
"You take your sled to work?"

"No. I sent for it after the nurse called
and said you were ready to escape. I had a
feeling you were going to be stubborn about
leaving and I wanted to be able to find you
if you did take off on your own. My parents
live on the far side of the village. It may be
small, but you'd hurt yourself if you tried to
swing your way there. Get on."

He couldn't argue that logic but his pride
took a beating all the same. He didn't want
to be carted through the village in the basket
of Holly's sled while she was in the driver's
stance.

Sexist or not, he was a man with an old-
fashioned attitude when it came to certain
things. Men opened doors for their women,
carried the heavy stuff—drove the sled. The
last thing he wanted to do was climb aboard
only to run into the sheriff along the way.

"Seriously? You're going to balk
now, over this?" Holly asked, her tone
incredulous. "You and Devon have more in
common than I thought."

He didn't like the comparison. "Just
getting my bearings."

"Uh-huh."

Something about her called to him. She was sass and fun and mischief, adventure, and he'd be lying if he said all of those qualities didn't appeal to him.

He eased into the snow, careful to make sure the rubber-tipped crutches would hold his weight before swinging himself forward. Maneuvering in the foot of fresh accumulation that shrouded the entry took some doing, but he made it to the sled and lowered himself into the basket.

Holly draped a blanket over him to keep him warm, her long hair falling forward and blowing into his face. It smelled nice, like cinnamon and vanilla and fresh snow.

"That should keep you warm enough until we get there."

Another gust sent her hair into his eyes and he brushed it away, winding it around his fingers before tucking it behind her ear. The strands were soft, and touching them made him want to bury his hands in the length. "Thanks."

"You're welcome," she said as she drew away. "I thought we would go the scenic route. Less visibility that way," she said, adding, "since you're obviously uncomfortable being the passenger."

He ignored the teasing. Less visibility worked for him.

The dogs were raring to go and the moment Holly gave the order, they dug in their paws and the sled jerked to a start.

Even taking the "scenic route" he could tell that the village was as small and unimpressive as Holly had indicated. There were fifteen to twenty cottages dotting the woods, scattered amongst the narrow paths. It was hard for him to get a good count because they blended into the pines and snow and scenery so well.

Beside the infirmary was what looked to be a general store, and beside that a school, if the colorful pictures hanging in the windows were any indication. But across a narrow street and down a ways, tucked deeper into the mountain in what appeared to be the center of the village, were two larger structures he couldn't identify. There were no pictures or signs, nothing to indicate their purpose. "What are those buildings there?" Ty asked, tilting his head back to see Holly's face.

"Just storage."

"Have you had some trouble?" he asked, spying two men out front.

On guard?

The men's bearing, their intensity, and the fact they were dressed in winter-colored camo like the sheriff made it clear they were there for a reason—and not mere deputies. Villages this size had a single law enforcement official, *if* they had one at all. No way did they have three.

"It's just a precaution. Nothing to worry about."

He wasn't worried—until she confirmed his suspicion that the men *were* guards and they weren't standing in the cold for a simple nicotine fix.

"They're there because I'm in the village? Because I left the infirmary?"

"Don't take it personally. You can see how isolated we are. It's a simple precaution, that's all."

Maybe. But the more she tried to explain away their presence the more alarms sounded in his head.

He'd been in plenty of villages where guards were placed outside fuel and food supplies. Outsiders were regarded as untrustworthy until they proved themselves. But he'd never seen small village guards like the ones here. They looked... organized and ready for anything.

Holly chose a path that took them away from the larger buildings. On purpose? To end the questions?

The ride got bumpy as they headed into the woods, then up a slope and round a curve.

A couple more minutes passed in silence, and he focused on the homes scattered so well amongst the trails that they would be next to impossible to locate from the air. *So well hidden.*

He remembered Holly's comment about living off-the-grid but there was off-the-grid—and hiding-in-plain-sight. Which were they?

"Here we are," Holly said.

Her parents' home was a simple cottage like the others, but larger than any of the rest he'd seen so far. Ty took in the details of the house as he painstakingly got to his feet and made his way across the slippery, packed snow to the porch.

Holly followed behind him, her hands lightly touching his back to add support and balance when he wobbled.

Ty felt more than one pair of eyes on him as he ascended the steps. Curious neighbors—or more guards keeping watch?

Finally he made it to the narrow porch and a blast of warm, cookie-scented air hit his face the moment Holly opened the door. He crossed the threshold, careful to step on the rug with his snow-covered boot.

Once he was on solid ground he lifted his head and barely managed to keep his surprise under control. He wasn't a man impressed by houses or antiques but—this was a first.

The interior looked like something out of a museum. A mix of old and new, the hall was filled with dark wood furniture gleaming from polish. The entry held a homey feel, with pictures of Holly at various stages decorating the walls and tables.

"You should get off that foot and warm up. The living room is closest," Holly said. "This way."

The living room looked like the entry. Every wall was decorated with shelves and clocks, pictures with thick, wide frames running from mid-wall to ceiling, old-looking snow globes and fancy dishes on display. On the far end was a massive fireplace fronted by a leather couch and recliner, a rocking chair, and on the opposite wall stretched loaded bookshelves with a seating area facing a baby grand that took center stage. If they didn't have supply drops, how had they gotten all of that here?

Just because they don't have supply drops now doesn't mean that was always the case.

"My mother's," Holly said when she noticed what had snagged his attention.

"This is quite a house."

Holly's smile looked more genuine this time, unlike the ones she'd tried to pass off earlier when he'd noticed the guards.

"Thanks. Every generation adds a little to the decor as you can probably tell."

"Your ancestors have been in the village how long?"

"Generations. Too many to count."

Which wasn't really an answer.

"Holly, dear," a woman said, bustling into the room carrying a loaded tray. "I heard you were bringing a guest. Sit down, both of you. I've brought something to warm you up."

The older woman was dressed in a hot pink, blinged-out tracksuit with an apron tied around her middle that read *Kiss the Cook*.

"Thank you, Anna. That's very thoughtful of you." Holly moved to the woman and dropped a kiss on her cheek. "Anna, this is Ty. Ty McGarretty, my aunt, Anna Belcher."

The woman wiped her hands on the apron before walking over to Ty, her hand extended.

"Nice to meet you." Anna gave him a firm shake, strong for someone her age. "Sit, sit. Holly, make our guest comfortable."

Holly tossed her coat aside and moved to stand before the fire, the snowflakes in her hair melting rapidly in the warmth of the house. Caught in the gold strands, the ice looked like sparkling crystals.

"I think if Ty wants to sit down, he will, Anna. Any of those cookies for me?"

"Oh, you. Enjoy that metabolism now. Our Holly could give the Cookie Monster a run for his cookies, she could," Anna said to Ty.

Ty smiled at Anna's bluster, liking the older woman and the image of Holly nibbling on cookies until her body was more lush and curvy than it already was.

"If you're in the mood to lecture, talk to Ty. He wanted to *walk* here."

"On crutches?" Anna said, managing to sound shocked and chiding in the same breath.

He winked at her. "A man has to keep moving to stay strong."

"Ooooh, would you listen to him, now. What kind of rascal have you brought into the house, Holly?"

Holly plopped down onto the leather couch, her white pants and turtleneck sweater looking like a dollop of cream in the middle of hot cocoa.

"I'm not sure, Anna. You'll have to help me keep him out of trouble, though."

"You," Anna said, pointing a finger at Ty, "sit down and get off of that foot. This should tide you over until dinner. I'm fixin' a pot roast and pie so don't eat too many of those cookies."

"Yes, ma'am," he said, nodding his agreement and earning an approving look from Anna.

Anna excused herself and went to check on her roast. Once she was gone Ty closed the distance between him and the couch, lowering himself down beside Holly. He was determined to make the best of a bad situation since he was stuck here and— There were definitely worse places to be stuck. "Anna seems fun."

Holly squirmed on the cushion before shoving herself to her feet and going back to the fire. "She is. Sometimes when I was growing up Anna acted more like the kid and I was the one reeling *her* in."

"That must have been a sight."

His words brought out one of Holly's throaty laughs.

"It was. Don't be too fooled. That sweet little old lady act is all for show. She's killer at checkers, and used to drive a sled team like nobody's business."

"Sled team?"

"Who do you think taught me?"

He smiled at the image. "Anything else I should know about your family?"

"Nothing in particular. Why?"

His mind flashed on the image of the guards outside the storage buildings and like it or not his knee-jerk reaction was that something else was going on here.

Winter had settled in and it looked to be a hard one. Food stores, fuel, supplies— it all had to be secured as a matter of survival. Maybe that knot on his head had done more damage than he thought, but for a place this isolated, who needed uniformed guards?

Focus on getting out of here. Nothing else. "Just wondering."

He watched as Holly helped herself to another cookie, his thoughts all over the place given what he'd seen on the way to her home.

The hidden cottages, the infirmary in a place he knew good and well wasn't on any map, no supply drops. Nothing to bring attention to them. But to be as well-appointed as it was...

Was this place a simple off-the-grid collection of loners who had banded together for survival, or something more? Some kind of militia group? That might explain the BDUs worn by Devon Sage and the guards because Ty seriously doubted them to be true law enforcement.

But if they were militia or some kind of secret sect...

That means you may have a harder time getting out of here than you thought.

CHAPTER FIVE

Y ou brought him into your father's home?" Devon growled. "*Holly.*"

Holly pushed Devon backward with a hand on his broad chest, crowding him into the swinging door separating the kitchen from the rest of the cottage. "*Shhhh.* He's asleep on the couch."

"I don't care if he's— Holly, what are you thinking?"

Holly stared up at Devon and wondered the same thing. But where else could she have taken Ty? "It wasn't like I had a lot of choices. I hate having him in my home." And the way Ty made her feel so aware of him. "But I brought him into our lives and I have to see this through."

"This is insane. Holly, I can't hide this from the elders. Do you know the position this will put your father in?"

She knew—and she didn't want to think about what would happen now. "Keeping Ty isolated here is the best solution, especially considering how he was about to walk out the infirmary door. Would you rather I let him wander around?"

Devon's face took on a dark purple hue.

"I'd rather you'd let me handle him the way I wanted from the beginning."

"We have to focus on him being here now. Did Jamie fill you in?"

Devon's nostrils flared as he inhaled. "Yes."

"Then you know exactly why Ty is here. Jamie has children at home. Alicia, too. If one of them said something... This house is secure. No business is ever conducted here. My mother sees to that."

Growing up, her mother had been adamant about her father not bringing work home with him. Birgit wanted their house to be a home, with the time her father spent there focused on their family and nothing else. This was the only place within the compound where she didn't

have to worry about Ty discovering
something he shouldn't.

"I can't believe you brought him here."

She had to dig deep for the patience
to keep her voice low. "Devon, it's not like
Ty can stay in the guard house with you.
Or do you want him to help you plan the
routes and check the security systems? I
won't screw up, and neither will Anna, and
you know good and well she is the perfect
chaperone—not that we need one," she
quickly added. "The snowstorm is supposed
to break tomorrow afternoon. I'll be packed
and ready to sled Ty out when everyone is at
Sunday service."

"Yeah, well, that's a good plan but you
can't."

"Why not?" Devon glared down into her
face but Holly glared right back, knowing
how much Devon didn't like it that she
wasn't the slightest bit intimidated by his
bluster.

She felt horrible about kissing Ty,
horrible about bringing him to the village
at all, but she couldn't undo the past and
sometimes when Devon looked at her—the
way he was right now—it reminded her of
when they were young, when Devon's glares

made her feel guilty for trouncing him at Monopoly. She wanted to be with someone who didn't make her feel bad for being who she was.

"The pass is closed," he said, his voice gruff. "The blizzard wiped out trails. Trees are down, too many to sled around. Unless he's able to hike it, no one is going anywhere for a while. Not until we can clear a way out."

She exhaled, at a loss for what to suggest next, only then noticing two duffles stacked behind Devon. "Are those Ty's?"

"His name is on them."

"Did you...?"

"Go through them? Yes."

"And? Did you find anything?" Ty seemed nice but she knew they had to be careful given the circumstances.

"Clothes and a DOP kit, a hand-carved cane that looks to be new, some native toys and art, a dead cell phone— and a handgun."

That made her grimace even though she wasn't sure why. "Well, it *is* Alaska. What? You're wearing a gun too."

Devon's jaw firmed before he pinched the bridge of his nose and squeezed.

The sight made her feel bad for giving him such a hard time, especially since she had created the stress Devon was presently experiencing. "Headache?"

"Yeah. Amazingly enough, I only get them when you're up to something."

"Ha-ha." She pushed her childhood friend over to the age-worn kitchen table and pulled out a chair. "Sit. I'll get you something for the headache."

"I'm keeping the gun."

"It's Ty's."

"Not while he's here."

"And the constitutional right to bear arms?" she asked, retrieving the basket of OTC meds from the cabinet. She dug until she found what she was looking for.

"Doesn't apply in the compound."

"How am I going to explain why you took his gun?"

"Simple. Village rules. Where's Anna?"

"She's working on Ty's room. I came to check on him when I heard you charging through the door like a bull moose."

Her description earned her another glare from him.

"Make sure Anna is with you at all times. Better yet, I'll sleep on the couch tonight."

Oh, like that would go over well. Talk about uncomfortable. "*No*. Ty isn't going to attack me."

"Known him that long, have you?"

It was true. In the scheme of things she knew nothing about Ty other than the basic information he had imparted, but when it came down to it she was the one keeping secrets.

"The grandfather wants to talk to him," Devon stated.

"I know. I saw the message earlier when I checked. I'm not surprised, though. Ty is his only family and responsible for his sister's children. Of course the man is concerned. Ty can use the private line here. The number won't be traceable and it will set his grandfather's mind at ease," she said, nodding to herself because it was a sound idea, one that would keep a search party from forming. If George McGarretty talked to Ty and knew his grandson was coming home soon, was only delayed, there was no reason to call in the officials.

"Has he asked any questions? Caused any trouble?" Devon asked.

She leaned her hips against the countertop. "He saw the guards today, outside the big buildings. Did you really think he wouldn't notice how they were dressed after seeing you and being told you're the sheriff?"

"They must have been out on a break, otherwise they would have been inside."

"I know, but it was still a mistake that shouldn't have occurred. I made an excuse, said they guarded the supplies and agreed they were there as a precaution due to his presence in the village. I figured the truth was better than trying to come up with another reason."

"Yes, well, we have a bigger issue to deal with. We're behind a shipment and it needs to be delivered. The storm delayed it but we have to keep things moving through the compound to get them in position."

But if Ty were here and he saw the flight-drop taking place... Oh, what were they going to do? Ty was getting antsy today after being cooped up in the hospital. He might make it the rest of the evening, maybe another day or two without much fuss, but if he heard or saw the plane?

"I'll have to come up with a plan to fix the mess you've gotten us into."

Devon's irritation was obvious.

But instead of the guilt she should probably feel, she frowned. What kind of cruel punishment was this? Being attracted to a man she couldn't have under any circumstances due to the legacy her family honored above all else—yet destined to spend her life working with a man who shared her goals and dreams but resented the power she'd wield? Someone who would fight her for control at every turn? "I can handle my own messes," she said. "Dev, lighten up. He's here. Deal with it."

"Lighten up? Holly, do you have *any idea* what you've done?"

"Yes! It's bad, but it's not the end of the world, Dev. See, this is why I *can't* be with you."

"What?" he asked, drawing back as though she'd slugged him.

"This—this attitude you have. You say you want me—"

"I do."

"But what you really want is to rule."

"We're arguing over nonsense just because he's here." Devon stared down at her, a frown pulling his thick eyebrows together into a sharp V.

Nonsense? She told him how she felt, the truth, and he called it *nonsense*? And what about his lack of response? She made the statement hoping he would deny the claim about him wanting to rule, but she wasn't hearing a denial from him. Not at all.

"You're not objective, Holly. And whether you'll admit it or not, everything was fine until you interfered in an area where *I* am the expert."

Another jab. "Well, now we both know where we stand, don't we?" After the day they had experienced and the pressure they were under, both were on edge. Snapping at each other wasn't helping. "Thank you for going after Ty's things," she said, putting an end to the conversation. "If Ty is still here when the drop takes place, Anna and I will think of some way to distract him."

Maybe they could blast the stereo, get a tree and force Ty to help them decorate? Something that would keep him busy?

"You'd better or I'll take care of him myself."

She rolled her eyes, refusing to be professional when Devon made comments like that. "Will you *stop* with the threats?" she ordered, her voice rough with her anger, low from the need to not be overheard. "You will not hurt him, Dev. My father wouldn't condone it and neither will I."

Devon stood, his damp boots squeaking on Anna's spotless floor as he pushed his chair in and rearranged the placemat he'd moved.

How could someone capable of such a kindness for Anna's sake be so unfeeling when it came to someone outside their organization?

"It would help if you weren't defending him with every breath."

"Your behavior is forcing me to," she countered.

He opened his mouth to speak but quickly closed it, releasing another deep sigh. "Shall I inform your father of this new development since I doubt he's aware of it?"

She didn't so much as blink. "No, he isn't."

"That's what I thought. Keep Anna with you and McGarretty out of the village," Devon ordered, bypassing her on the way to the door. "Otherwise I'll do *whatever* is necessary to fix what you've done."

"You will *not* ignore my direct order."

Devon stopped just shy of the exit and turned to meet her gaze, his fury at her pulling rank banked but visible in the golden glow of his brown eyes.

"As you wish."

He opened the door and a cold blast of air swept through the kitchen, strong enough to lift her hair and blow it back over her shoulders.

But it was nothing like the cold blast spiraling through her body, chilling her from the inside out.

***

When Ty woke up that evening he found himself alone. He took a few minutes to shake off the groggy daze of sleep and grabbed his crutches, following the noises he heard from within the kitchen.

Anna bustled about fixing dinner and the moment she saw him the elderly woman invited him to join her while they waited on Holly to return from work.

Ty took a seat at the massive butcher block island, feeling as though he was back in his grandmother's house in New York.

He apologized for falling asleep so rudely, and then he and Anna talked about news events and happenings in Anchorage and around the world, general stuff that people stuck in isolated places wanted to get caught up on.

After a while his foot began to throb because it wasn't propped up. Anna noticed, ordered him back to the couch, and brought him a selection of bestselling novels to keep himself entertained. Someone in the house was a mystery buff and fan of sci-fi.

An hour or so into a story about a deep space cowboy he heard a door open somewhere in the house and listened, recognizing Holly's voice greeting Anna.

"Hey," Holly said, pushing through the swinging door into the main room. "You're awake."

"Yeah. Sorry about that."

She looked tired. Or sad. Maybe a little of both.

"No need to apologize. You're still recovering. I'd be surprised if you didn't fall asleep."

"Well, I'm awake now. Work went okay for you? You weren't away too long?"

"No, it was fine. My schedule is flexible so long as the job gets done," she said with a shrug.

"Looks like you brought some of it home with you."

Holly patted the bulging tote bag she carried. "Just some reading I need to catch up on. I thought I might work while you rest."

Anna entered the room behind Holly and the older woman *tsked* at Holly's statement.

"You shouldn't have brought that home," Anna said sternly.

"It's fine, Anna. After all, I can't be in two places at once."

Ty frowned at her wording and the intense look the two women exchanged.

"Yes, well, you are allowed a day off every now and again," Anna chided. "Let me have that. I'll put it in your room for safekeeping while you help Ty to the table and get seated. Dinner's almost ready."

Ty scooted to the edge of the couch and shoved himself to his feet. Waiting for him at the eight-person table, Holly pulled out a chair and waited with a snarky grin when he raised his eyebrows at the role reversal. "You're enjoying this, aren't you?"

"Li'l bit, yeah."

He seated himself but before she could step away, he used one of his crutches to shove the chair closest to him away from the table. "Never let it be said I'm not resourceful."

"And obviously a gentleman," Anna added, returning to the room.

Despite his anxiousness to get back to Anchorage, Ty enjoyed dinner. When he ate with Gramps and the kids conversations often lacked certain things—like points, sense, and manners. Random topics appeared out of nowhere and were often accompanied by farts and burps. Abbie was one of the worst culprits, seemingly timing her performances to get the maximum amount of laughs.

Here conversation topics ranged from the weather to favorite foods to the places he had traveled and the destinations he still wanted to see.

An hour or so after dinner was cleaned up, Anna set her knitting aside and claimed fatigue, turning in for the night.

Ty sat in the recliner with his foot propped up, while Holly took the corner of the couch and stared into the fire burning in the hearth. He watched her for a while, curious as to what had her so pensive. "Everything okay?"

She blinked away the dazed expression and managed a weak smile. "Yeah. Fine. Just thinking."

"Barney knows I'm here now, huh?" She glanced up in surprise and Ty knew he'd guessed correctly. "Did he give you a hard time?"

Holly looked down at the untouched mug of eggnog in her hands. "Devon is worried that you're in our home, that's all. He did do you a favor, though. He brought your bags from the plane. They're by the door in the kitchen."

He was glad to have them back in his possession but he hated to be indebted to the sheriff. "I'll be sure to say thanks the next time I see him."

"He, um, kept your gun." Holly exhaled, shifting sideways on the couch. "Just so you know."

"He searched my belongings?" If he needed another sign that he needed to get out of the village as soon as possible, that was it. He had a concealed carry permit, and he'd been trained by the military on proper gun use. Who were they to go through his things and confiscate his weapon just because he'd crashed into their super-secret valley? What was going on here?

"Don't be offended, please. It's just a precaution. You'll get the weapon back when you leave."

Which couldn't happen soon enough. "When will that be?" he asked.

Several expressions flickered across her face, none of them looking very promising.

"Not as soon as you probably hope. The mountain pass is closed, and it's the only way in and out. You're stuck here until some of the men can clear the pass enough that I can sled you out."

He was trapped, unarmed, and injured? Completely at their mercy?

Ty reminded himself that they had traveled home in the snow earlier and he'd seen the depth of the new accumulation. The higher elevations would be even worse. He couldn't fault them for nature but more alarm bells went off in his head, the little hairs at the base of his neck prickling.

"Ty, this is a temporary setback. Please, be patient. As soon as the men get the paths cleared, I'll see to it that you get home. You have my word."

And he had to take her word at face value, just like he had to accept the village at face value. For now. "I think I'm going to turn in, too." He grabbed his crutches and stood, moving toward the hallway that would lead him to the bedroom Holly and Anna had shown him earlier. On the way he passed the hearth, the photos atop the mantle above it snagging his attention.

Holly looked like her mother. Blond, blue-eyed, beautiful. In the impromptu snapshot Holly looked to be a teenager, more eyes and legs and hair than anything. They were in a kitchen, cookie dough rolled out in front of them. Both wore smiles and aprons, cutting shapes to place on a baking sheet.

Another photo was of Holly and Anna standing beside a dog sled team. Another of Holly and— A laugh erupted from his chest. Seriously?

"What's so funny?" Holly asked, still seated on the couch.

Ty pointed to the photo. "Who's that?"

"My father."

No wonder she had blue eyes. The man in the photo smiled at the camera, his deep blue eyes twinkling. He wore a black Harley-Davidson Mumbai T-shirt over a thermal and camo pants like those Ty had seen around the camp, suspenders fitted around a good-sized belly. "You don't think he resembles anyone?"

Holly got up and moved toward him.

"He looks like my uncle Richard."

"Holly, come on. The white hair and beard? You have to admit all your dad needs is a red suit and he'd make one heck of a great mall Santa."

"Ooooh," she said, crossing her arms over her chest, her laughter emerging a little high-pitched, "yeah. He gets that a lot, especially this time of year."

Holly left the hearth to gather the mugs and return them to a tray on the coffee table.

"I'm going to clean these up before I go to my room. You're settled for the night?"

"Yeah, I'm fine. Anna showed me the towels and everything earlier."

"Great. Well, I guess I'll see you in the morning. Goodnight, Ty."

Holly hesitated for a moment before she carried the tray to the kitchen.

Was it his imagination or was that last smile a little too cheerful? Too tense? Forced?

When the swinging door closed behind her, Ty looked back at the photograph. Man, the resemblance was just weird. But even funnier?

Was realizing he was more than a little attracted to *Santa's* secretive daughter.

CHAPTER SIX

Immediately after an early morning breakfast Holly sent Anna off to church in the village while she went to the kennel to feed and care for her dogs, leaving a note for Ty on the kitchen counter that his breakfast was in the oven.

She hated to miss the service but it was too dangerous to leave Ty alone and more dangerous, still, to take him to church.

She took out her pent up frustrations on the dog pens, cleaning them, her thoughts full of Devon and Ty and how something as simple as doing the right thing had become so overwhelmingly complicated.

Take the work she had brought home, for instance. She knew her mother's

rules for carting work into the house
and yet she'd done it anyway. A reckless,
thoughtless, impromptu gesture she
blamed entirely on her reaction to Devon's
attitude—and her determination to...what?
Prove herself?

If something happened and Ty found
out the truth, if he connected the lists of
names and dates to certain events in the
outside world?

The Elder Council would have a lot more
ammunition with which to condemn her.

In for a penny, in for a pound.

Moxie finished her breakfast and left
her stall, padding toward her and sitting at
Holly's feet.

Holly patted the dog, lowering herself
to the floor of the kennel so she could
hug Moxie and lean against her sturdy
frame. "Mox, what am I going to do?
What am I thinking, huh? Why him?
Why am I interested in *him* instead of...
one of us?" She stared into the dog's pale
blue eyes, scratching behind Moxie's ears
just the way she liked. "I know what I
want. What I'd love to have one day. But
I'm beginning to think it's impossible.
That it doesn't exist for me. Anna and

Mama would say to wait on God's timing. I know that's exactly what I should do, but…."

After all if Devon, whom she had known all of her life was interested in her even partially for the power she would one day inherit, how could she ever trust anyone else? Know that if and when she met someone they wanted *her*, not the legacy she carried?

∗∗∗

An hour later the door to the kennel opened. Holly looked up to find Ty standing in the entry, his tall frame silhouetted by the blowing wall of white behind him. The snowstorm raged on, each and every flake adding to the problem they faced of having Ty in the village. "What are you doing out here? What if you'd fallen walking from the house?"

Ty closed out the cold and swung his way toward the open stall where she sat on a thick layer of blankets.

"I came to see what was keeping you and to share my good news."

She indicated the dogs lying all around her and over her lap and legs with a wave of her hand. "Now you know. What's your good news?"

"The swelling went down enough that I was able to get my boot on."

Oh, so he had. She hadn't noticed. Why look at the man's foot when there was so much else to take in?

She shoved the pile of dogs off her and got to her feet. Spending time in the cold and the kennel went a long way to help clear her head. She'd had a strict talk with herself about her thoughts regarding Ty, but now that he stood in front of her all the warnings went out the window.

"That's some heating system you have there."

"The best. A good musher spends time with their animals no matter the weather. How I take care of them is how they will take care of me out there," she said, waving toward the door. "Guys, time for bed. Bed," she repeated firmly, clapping her hands together twice.

The dogs took off down the aisle of the kennel, going into their respective pens without trouble.

Ty whistled. "Whoa. Wish the kids were that well behaved."

She laughed and began latching the individual doors. "From what I've seen most children do not appreciate the rules of bedtime."

Ty helped latch the pen doors closest to him. "Got that right."

Something flickered across his features, catching Holly's attention. "You okay?"

"Yeah."

"That's not very convincing. Something to do with... Beth?"

A wry smile formed on Ty's lips. "Very perceptive."

"I've been told I'm a good listener, just so you know." She waited, hoping to gain some insight into his thoughts.

Ty latched another of the gates. "I just wonder why it had to be her," he said softly. "The kids need her. Way more than they need me or Gramps."

Realization dawned and she inhaled, thinking she and Ty had quite a bit in common. "You're worried you're going to screw up," she said softly.

He turned his head, his green eyes searching hers. "Wouldn't you be worried if you were suddenly a parent? Those kids have been hurt enough."

Holly moved to another gate, giving Jo-Jo a good scratch behind his ears. "I think that's where faith comes in," she said, reminding herself that she needed to practice what she preached. "You have to do the best you can at the time and pray it's enough. What else can you do?"

The words were easy to say but hard to swallow when it came to herself. Wasn't that always the case, though? Sometimes she really wondered if she had what it took to handle her father's business considering all aspects involved, but on other days she felt she was ready. More than ready. The constant back-and-forth was enough to drive her batty, making her wish for more confidence. A feeling that told her without a doubt that she was prepared to lead her people into the future.

Once all the dogs were taken care of, she and Ty left the kennel to return to the house. Halfway up the narrow path she glanced behind her to discover Ty had stopped outside the kennel and stood tall and still, face lifted to the falling snow.

The peacefulness of the moment hit her like a tidal wave. Soft breeze, big, fluffy flakes. Strong, utterly beautiful man.

Her mind instantly captured the moment. The cant of his head, the angle of

Kay Lyons Stockham

his jaw. The masculine appeal of his dark hair and broad-shouldered form that sucked her in like a whirlpool.

"Holly, come here for a sec."

Curious, she retraced her steps, drawn to the husky rumble of his voice. "Something wrong?"

Ty lowered his chin from the sky and smiled at her, the lines around his mouth deepening.

"What?" she said, smiling back because she couldn't seem to help herself.

"When was the last time you took some time out of your busy day to make a snow angel?"

That was all the warning she got before he reached out with both hands and gently shoved her backward into the drift lining the shoveled path.

Holly shrieked in surprise but the moment her back and butt hit the snow she laughed. "Oh, you are so going to pay for that!" she yelled, scrambling for handfuls of snow to throw at him.

Ty's chuckle echoed off the house and kennel as he grabbed for snow. "Bring it, sweetheart. Nothing surprises bush pilots— and you throw like a girl."

Twenty minutes later Ty declared the snowball fight a draw. He had gotten in a few good shots but so had she, one of which landed on the back of Ty's neck and slid down his coat. She considered that the tie-*breaker.*

After doing her victory dance Holly dropped back into the snow and began pumping her arms and legs, making the snow angel she hadn't made earlier due to the fact she'd been heart-set on extracting revenge.

Surprisingly Ty tossed his crutches aside and did the same, falling into the snow and making his own angel before snagging her hand during one of the swipes so that the "angels" touched.

The gesture was sweet and silly and insanely thrilling, for something so simple.

They managed to get to their feet without doing too much damage to their angels, dusting themselves off as the cold drove them inside.

"Any word on the phone situation? I'd like to call Gramps." Ty unzipped his coat and hung it on a peg to dry, pulling off his hat next. "Think you could check on the status and let me know what's happening?"

"Sure," she said, her gaze meeting the newly arrived Anna's across the kitchen.

"Actually, I saw Devon on my way to church this morning. He said the village should be able to get calls out for a short period this afternoon. Something to do with the power and the generator," Anna explained to Ty, doing a good job at looking clueless as to the process even though Anna knew full well how things worked.

Given the situation Holly knew someone, somewhere, would be monitoring Ty's call. There would also be a delay in the transfer, allowing any information such as names, location, and so forth to be blocked with a burst of static.

"If you want to try now, Holly and I will start lunch. We wouldn't want your grandfather worrying needlessly."

Holly left the room long enough to remove the Sat-phone from where she had hidden it with the work she'd brought home. She returned to the kitchen, punching in the code that would connect Ty before handing it over. "Anna's right. It's working. Just input your number. Be sure he knows you're okay."

"Thanks," Ty said, his gaze warm on hers.

Ty left one crutch propped against the island and used the other to make his way through the swinging door.

"Quit your fretting," Anna scolded softly. "Devon is waiting and ready to intercede if need be."

Of course he was.

Holly crossed to the coffee pot and poured herself a small portion, adding a larger measure of hot chocolate. "Devon shouldn't be the one eavesdropping."

"Oh? Why's that?"

Realizing she'd just stuck her foot in her mouth without meaning to, Holly sipped her concoction and scorched her tongue in the process. "Ow."

"Careful, dear. Now what did you mean?"

"Nothing."

"Now, now. Is there something going on that I should know about?" Anna opened the refrigerator and retrieved a container of whipped topping and chocolate shavings already prepared.

Holly added a dollop of topping to her mug as well as a spoonful of chocolate shavings sprinkled over the top. "Just thinking aloud."

"I don't suppose this has anything to do with Ty being here?"

"You know it has *everything* to do with Ty. And don't pretend you like Ty being here. I know you don't."

"It's true I wasn't expecting to enjoy his company but I haven't found it as difficult as I'd thought. And I will say that Ty is a handsome man. He would make any woman's heart go aflutter, young or old but—"

"But he's an outsider," Holly said, needing to say the words aloud.

It took her several seconds before she realized she'd touched on a sore subject with Anna and reached out to wrap an arm around her aunt's shoulders. "I'm sorry."

"It's fine."

"No, it's not. I know better than to talk about the outside with you and here I am not only doing that, but bringing Ty to stay with us. Oh, Anna, I've screwed everything up and hurt you in the process."

"You haven't hurt me, dear."

She stared into Anna's gentle, kind eyes and sighed. "Have you heard from Ben?" she asked, referring to Anna's son. Ben was seven years older than Holly and a doctor in Ohio.

"Yes. He and Zoey are expecting."

"That's wonderful!"

Anna nodded her agreement but the tears in her eyes relayed her sadness because— Because she would never be able to see them. Her son, her grandchild. Grand*children*.

Because of the rules.

Now that Ben had left, he wasn't allowed to return. "Oh, Anna."

Anna wiped her eyes with a tissue pulled from her sleeve. "I knew it was coming. That it was only a matter of time. Ben was so sad after his father died, I knew he needed a change. To go somewhere different. I just didn't think he'd stay o-or choose someone there."

Her cousin had begged her father for a chance to go to medical school, promising to return to the village to practice. But right before the time came for him to return, Ben had met Zoey, another med student and an outsider, and Ben had been forced to make a decision.

Holly hugged Anna and tried to offer comfort.

It was wrong. For those who chose to stay here, to follow through on their upbringing and family tradition, they were the ones who suffered. They were the ones who had to sacrifice and hide. To give up physical contact with family members who left because of something that happened how long ago?

"The internet is a wonderful thing," Anna said. "Ben promised to send pictures, and video clips."

"That's wonderful." But it wasn't the same as holding her grandchild in her arms.

Anna patted her eyes with the tissue one last time.

"Tell me why Devon shouldn't be the one listening to Ty. What's going on? And no more fibs."

"I think Devon is...jealous."

"Of?"

Oh, this wasn't going to go over well. "I kissed Ty."

"*Holly Elizabeth Klaas.*"

Holly held up her hands in complete surrender. "It was a mistake, I know. Please don't lecture."

Anna left the bag of frozen corn on the counter and moved closer to where Holly stood.

"You realize Ty is leaving. That he *has* to leave."

Did Anna really think that thought was ever far from mind? Ty had only been there a matter of days. How was it even possible to feel so much in such a short amount of time? About a man she'd only recently met? "Of course."

"And you know the consequences of choosing that life."

"I'm not choosing *that* life. I'd never give up my home, not for anyone."

"Thank goodness for that. You've given me a scare," Anna said, putting her hand over her heart and patting several times. "I've lost one child to that world. I couldn't bear to lose another. And your mama and papa. Oh, they would be heartbroken."

"Yeah, well, I'm sure Papa will be heartbroken anyway when I tell him I am definitely not interested in Devon and never will be. I've let things slide thinking maybe one day I'd feel something more for Devon but it's not going to happen. He'll always be a friend but nothing more."

"Your papa will understand. The good news is that you're young. You have plenty of time to decide these things. Maybe you should go with your father on his next trip, meet some new men within the organization. I know your mother would like the company. She gets lonely while your father is in meetings all day."

It was a good idea. And while she hated to be calculating about her reasons for accompanying her father, doing so would serve to give her some time and breathing room away from the village. Not to mention it would give her more experience in dealing with her future responsibilities. *And be a distraction from what's happening now?* "I think I will. I'll bring it up when Papa comes home." She hugged Anna again. "Thank you."

"For what?"

"For just being you. I doubt my parents would have been quite so understanding."

***

"Ty-Ty come home?" Abbie said in her babyish voice.

Ty closed his eyes and pictured his niece in his head. "I'll be home as soon as I can, sweetheart. You be good for Gramps, okay?"

"Ty-Ty come home now."

"Soon," he promised, hating the way her voice thickened with tears.

"Pwease?"

Oh, man. When she grew up the girl was going to have men wrapped around her little finger. "Sweetie, I'll be there as soon as I can, okay? I promise. Can I talk to Gramps now?"

"No."

Ty heard Gramps telling Abbie that her bunny was hungry and needed her.

"You there?" Gramps asked.

"Yeah. Gramps, I'm sorry you're dealing with this on your own."

"I'm just grateful you'll be coming home," Gramps said, his voice gruff.

Gramps had a few questions about the crash and the weather, more confirming the kids' routine, before bursts of static made them end the call.

Ty felt a little better after his conversation with Gramps. So far the kids were fine, though Gramps sounded tired but in decent spirits.

But something had changed with Holly while he was on the phone with Gramps.

When he returned to the main part of the house Holly had asked if Gramps and the kids were okay, then avoided attempts to make small talk, preferring instead to keep her nose buried in a binder of work she studied while seated at a desk in the far corner of the living room.

Ty sat in the recliner with his foot propped up, and alternated between reading and trying to be discreet as he stared at Holly.

Some men might take his present situation with the kids and his interest in Holly and turn it into a reason to want more, maybe even settle down. For the kids' sake.

But while the thought had merit, his bitterness over his mother's adulterous behavior during his formative years, combined with his suspicions about Holly and her village, made it clear. Holly wasn't the woman for him.

But seeing Holly in the kennel surrounded by her dogs? Laughing in the snow as she'd pumped her arms and legs to make an angel? Just when he thought he had a handle on things he found himself sucker punched by a whole new wave of attraction. Her personality was at odds with the thoughts he held about the compound and all the secrets. Still, his gut told him something big was happening here.

By nine o'clock that evening he'd finished the book and found the second in the series in the stack Anna had brought him. He set it aside for later, his gaze drawn back to Holly.

Her head was bent over the bound paper, her hair falling forward across her cheek. She had a pen in one hand and every now and again she would make a notation on the sheets. "Sure I can't give you a hand? I'm pretty good with numbers."

His comment stemmed from his desire to get a look at whatever it was she studied so thoroughly.

"No. Actually I'm done for the day. My eyes are crossing."

"We're a pair then," Anna said. "I'm nodding off and about to poke myself with my needle." Anna lowered the mass of knitting and tools into a basket by her chair. "Holly, are you going into work tomorrow or staying here?" The elderly woman glanced at Ty. "With her father out of the village she has a lot to do. Maybe it's best if you go in," Anna urged. "You know how that place gets when you're not there."

Holly maintained eye contact with her aunt for a long moment before she blinked and closed the binder with a nod. "I probably should go in and check on things."

Ty closed his book as well. "My offer stands if I can help. It's the least I can do for you giving me room and board."

"There's nothing for you to do," Holly said. "But thanks for the offer."

"And hospitality isn't something that should have to be purchased," Anna added. "Besides, the storm is winding down. You need to rest as much as possible. Won't be long before the pass is cleared and you'll be on your way."

Was that said to make a point?

Ty split his attention between Anna and Holly and quickly decided Anna was reminding Holly that he wasn't here to stay. But why was the warning necessary unless...?

Holly's interested in him?

Was his ego getting in the way of clear thinking? Had Holly said something to make Anna think her niece *needed* the reminder?

Screwed up or not, the thought had him sitting up a bit in the chair.

"She's right," Holly said, putting the binder into the tote bag she'd carried home from work. "You'll need to be at your best when the time comes. The journey won't be easy, even riding in the sled."

"I'll be fine."

"So you are going to work?" Anna asked, bringing them back to their original topic.

"Yes. Otherwise I won't have my reports ready when Papa returns."

Reports for what? What could they be doing in this tiny little village that would require such a strict schedule? "What does your father do again?"

"He's a consultant."

He raised his eyebrows at that. "A consultant who lives here? In the middle of no-man's land?"

Holly nodded and busied herself by gathering up her pens and notepads. "Now you understand why he has to travel so much." She closed the laptop and added it to the tote before she stood, carrying it with her and even pausing to make sure she'd left nothing behind. "Goodnight, Anna. Ty."

"Goodnight," he said.

Holly held his gaze for a long moment before disappearing down the hall.

Anna hesitated and it took him a second to realize why. He held the second book up for her to see. "I'm going to read for a little while longer if you don't mind. I'll turn off the lights when I go to bed."

"Sleep well, then. Goodnight."

Anna walked to the desk Holly had vacated and rearranged a few skewed objects, making sure all was perfect before she left the room.

Another check to make sure nothing had been left behind?

Ty sat and stared into the banked fire for a long while, torn between duty and the weight of his responsibility where his family was concerned.

He inhaled and settled himself deeper into the cushions of the couch, focusing his attention on the hearth, his gaze drawn to the picture of her father on the mantle. The man didn't *look* like a criminal. But that whole thing about him being a consultant...

They thought he would buy a line like that?

Everyone doing something they shouldn't be doing called themselves some sort of consultant. *Shipping and receiving. Import-Export. Transportation Director.*

Whatever the title it was usually the same old game.

The story had to be bogus. A consultant for what? How? There was no decent phone service, no supply flights. Apparently no easy access into and out of the village. He still didn't know the *name* of the village.

The story was too far-fetched. Didn't mean Holly's father was doing something illegal but why lie about it if whatever he did was on the up-and-up?

You have other things to worry about. The kids, keeping your business afloat when you don't have a plane. Getting out of here without Devon-the-sheriff preventing it. Open a can of worms and you'd better be sure you're ready to face the fallout.

Thanks to his mother's infidelity, he'd learned to spot deception from an early age and he knew one thing for certain—Holly, Anna, the entire village, had a very, *very* big secret.

CHAPTER SEVEN

The next morning Ty came to awareness slowly. Small things registered first. The old-fashioned clock *tick-tocking* nearby. The chill in the room. The soft, warm body pressed against his side.

He opened his eyes and blinked, his gaze focusing on the ceiling. He was in the Klaas living room. With Holly?

He'd fallen asleep on the couch but woke around 4 a.m. when Holly had joined him, unable to sleep and on her way to the kitchen for a mug of hot chocolate. They had wound up watching an old black-and-white movie with the sound turned off. Holly had hit the mute button on accident and then couldn't find the remote so they'd smothered their laughter while making up their own dialogue.

"*Ahem.*"

Ty froze, feeling like a teenage boy caught kissing his first girl. He turned his head to find the older woman standing near the couch. "Good morning, Anna."

"Good morning to you, Mr. McGarretty. Sleep well?"

He shrugged off his embarrassment and grinned. He and Holly were fully clothed and nothing had happened between them, but it was still the best sleep he'd gotten in a while. "Yeah, as a matter of fact, I did."

"Ooh, listen to you," the woman said, wagging a finger at him. "Brazen, that's what you are. And at my Holly's expense."

"We fell asleep watching TV, Anna. That's all."

Holly stirred and rubbed her face in a sleepy gesture before lifting her head. "Mmmm. *Oh.* Oh, I'm sorry. What— What time is it?" she asked, visibly fighting to wake herself.

"Time for you to be on your way, Holly Elizabeth," Anna said, her tone filled with unmistakable disapproval. "You have a lot to do at work today."

Holly jerked her head up, her cheeks turning bright red as she glanced from him to Anna and back to him again.

"Of course. Th-thank you, Anna."

Once Anna shuffled off, Holly's breath left her chest in a rush and she buried her face into her hand once more, her shoulders quaking with muffled laughter.

"I'm *so* sorry. I can't believe I fell asleep on you. And then to wake up to Anna... Oh, I can only imagine the lecture that awaits both of us."

He nudged Holly's face up so he could see her. "It's fine."

Would there ever be a moment when Holly wasn't beautiful to him? Even sleep tousled and somewhat panicked over her aunt finding them snuggled together on the couch, all he could think about was the sweet sound of her laughter. The way it lit up her eyes.

Holly wasn't so bold and brazen now. He liked her flustered and with a blush on her cheeks. "Thanks for keeping me company last night." Without thought, he leaned forward and pressed a light, chaste kiss on her lips. A kiss even old Anna couldn't disapprove of too much.

After several long seconds, Holly pulled away, pushing herself fully upright on the couch. "Ty, I—I can't," she said.

"Because of the sheriff?"

"*No.* Definitely not. I just— Ty, my life is here and yours is out there."

He blinked at her and the way she had phrased her words. "Wait a second. You're saying no because I'm not from here?"

"It's village rules," she said simply. "I told you. We're off-the-grid and we like it. The rules are in place to keep our community as private and secluded as possible."

"But I'm here. I know about it now."

"Why do you think Devon is so angry with me?" she said. "Ty, if what just happened *wasn't* just a kiss and I were to choose you, I'd have to leave. I wouldn't be able to come home because I'd be... banished."

Banished? "That's archaic. I thought only the Amish did stuff like that."

"It's the way we live. For our protection."

Ty stayed close, staring into her blue eyes. "Protection from what?" He wanted to leave at the first opportunity but if his being here placed Holly in danger... How could he take off not knowing if she would be safe?

"Worldly things, ideas, negativity. Look, just never mind, okay?"

"No, it's not okay. What about your father?" he pressed. "He's away right now. The rules don't apply to him?"

"He's visiting a sister-village."

"So he can travel and the rest of you can't?"

"It's complicated. Just forget I said anything. It was just a good morning kiss, right? I'm overreacting."

Ty fingered a thick locket of her hair that had fallen over her shoulder, trying to absorb what she said. "Don't slug me for saying this if I'm wrong but is this some sort of commune? A polygamist group? Is Anna really your aunt?"

For the first time since their conversation began, an amused smile flitted about Holly's lips. "No, we're not a cult or a commune or a polygamist group. And, yes, she is my father's sister. When her husband died she chose to live with us and offer her cottage to a family who needed it."

Offered. Not sold?

"I have to go. I'm going to be late for work," Holly said, shoving herself to her feet.

"Holly…?" She paused and turned to face him, hesitation etched across her features.

"What?"

"It was a *good* kiss," he told her, the knot in his gut tightening when color rose in her cheeks once more.

She didn't comment at first. She simply inhaled and smoothed her hair from her face. "You should rest. That way you'll be well enough to go home when the time comes."

Holly ate lunch at her desk and kept working, refusing to let herself think about how it had felt to wake up in Ty's arms.

By dinner she knew she couldn't put off the inevitable. She'd have to face Ty and Anna sometime, and deal with the looks and lectures and warnings she knew her aunt would dish out.

The village was mostly quiet as she left her building for home. She could have taken one of the snowmobiles but the night was crisp and clear, and she needed the crunch of the snow beneath her boots to drive the chaos from her mind.

As she passed the guardhouse she heard the deep rumbling voices of the men and it reminded her of her childhood, running into her father's office and climbing into his big chair, happy because she knew one day it would be hers.

Some people hated this part of the year because of the twenty-four hour darkness but as she walked home she was reminded of all the walks she'd taken along the trails with her family. From the time she was potty-trained her father had begun taking her to work, teaching her.

Why would anyone risk losing what she had?

They wouldn't. That was the point.

But all day her stomach had been tied in knots because one minute she would be working and thinking of the changes she would make when she was fully in charge, and the next she remembered the man waiting for her at home. The way Ty talked to her, looked at her.

There's someone else for you. God wouldn't be so cruel as to let you fall for an outsider.

She frowned at the twinkling stars overhead, the moon almost full. In front of her on the trail she heard some of the village children laughing as they skated on the shallow pond built for just that reason.

Holly paused to watch the children, noting the grace and dexterity one little girl possessed. Mari's daughter?

The child was small and lithe, breathtakingly graceful. Full of potential as she twirled and spun and performed, lost in the magic of the moon.

Talent that won't do her any good here.

The thought stole her breath. Angered her. Enough that she stumbled over the snow, needing to get away from the sadness of the child never having the *opportunity* to see where her gift might lead.

Holly chose the longest roundabout trail that would take her deeper into the woods to home, needing some time to compose herself. She was cold and winded by the time she approached the cottage but rather than go inside, she let herself into the kennel.

The dogs heard her coming and barked, jumping at their gates. She released them all and ignored the fact she wore good clothes, dropping onto her blankets to play with her animals.

This was her home. Her future. Her calling.

But that little girl? If she chose to pursue skating she would have to shatter her heart and the hearts of all who loved her…

By the time Holly made it into the cottage her toes were numb.

"About time you came in," Anna chided. "I was beginning to think I was going to have to come after you."

Holly took off her coat and gloves, meeting Anna's gaze while unwrapping the scarf Anna had given her to replace the one ruined with Ty's blood from the night of the crash. "The dogs needed to play. They need a run. They're getting antsy."

"They're not the only one. That one's about to climb the walls," Anna said, indicating the kitchen door with a wave of her fingers. "He's read all three books in the series your father raved about, reorganized the movie cabinet, changed a few light bulbs I couldn't reach and took out the trash."

"Impressive."

Anna nodded her agreement, continuing to peel the potatoes in front of her. "He's in the middle of *Die Hard II* now."

"Thanks for the warning."

"So what have you done today besides hide in your office?"

"Wow, Anna, nice lead in," she said, leaning her hips against the countertop.

Anna pointed the knife at Holly. "Don't tell me you're not avoiding me after what I walked in on this morning. How can I not be worried about you after you told me you kissed him? To spend the night together…"

"*Nothing* happened. I got up for a drink and we wound up watching a movie that bored us to sleep. But sleep is all we did." Holly moved to wash her hands in the sink and opened the fridge to scrounge around. "It wasn't intentional, Anna."

"Your dinner is in the stove. I kept a plate warm for you."

"Thanks."

"Almost done with potatoes," Anna murmured. "Gonna have to sit through the onions if you don't start talking soon. Or is that the plan? Do you need to shed some tears, dear, and don't want it to be obvious?"

Holly wrinkled her nose. Onions were not her favorite. "Save the onions for when I'm not here, please. Yes, I was avoiding you," she said voluntarily, "because I needed some time to think."

"About?"

"Do you want the truth or for me to say what you want to hear?"

"Oh, Holly. Do I need to tell you again how much I miss my Ben? How my heart breaks every single day that he's not here?"

"*No.* And you don't need to worry about me, either. Ty and I are...I don't know. Friends, I suppose? But nothing else," she said with a shake of her head.

"And that's why you were sneaking around last night?"

"If we'd been *sneaking* you wouldn't have found us— And we were fully clothed."

"Oh, my girl."

Holly held up her left hand in surrender. "I know. It *looked* bad," Holly said, rounding the counter to kiss Anna's cheek. "But stop worrying. Please. Nothing happened."

Falling asleep watching television with Ty *had* been innocent. It was what came later, in her dreams, that wasn't.

Because it was so easy to imagine more with Ty. To let her head be filled by fantasies about dating him, about future winters with him there beside her, watching movies, making snow angels, and talking.

"I'm not blind, Holly. I see the way you two look at each other."

It was that obvious? Really? "Relationships can't be built on lies." She lowered her voice. "Nothing can happen between us when I can't tell Ty the truth."

Holly escaped the kitchen before Anna brought out the onions. She downed her dinner in the dining room and was curled up on the couch in front of the fire when Ty entered the living room on his crutches, a box tucked high beneath his arm.

"Hey. Welcome home."

"Thanks."

"You always work such long hours?"

She raised a knee to her chest and looped her arms around her leg. "I've been home for a while, actually. I was in the kennel."

Ty's gaze narrowed on her face and she blinked at the intensity before shifting her focus to the box he carried. She didn't want to get into it with him, not when nothing had changed and wouldn't. "You've switched from books to puzzles?"

He dropped down onto the couch beside her and she fought the immediate draw of his body. His size and warmth brought her comfort, his scent… He smelled of woods and pine and spices that made her think of the outdoors.

But *why* him? What was it about him?

"I finished reading the series. Thought I'd try something different."

She watched as he dumped the puzzle pieces onto the surface of the coffee table and began flipping them over. Deciding to dig herself out of her not-so-great mood, she slid to the floor beside the table and pitched in. "Did Anna tell you I like puzzles?"

"She may have mentioned it when I asked about the collection in there."

This particular puzzle was one of her favorites, a fact proven by the worn corners of the box. The image was of a beach, two sets of footprints in the sand, waves rolling into shore and big boulders in the distance, blocking the way to an even better, wider, prettier beach on the other side. Getting to that better beach was obviously a challenge but the view was worth the effort.

"Holly, listen. About this morning..."

"I'd rather not talk about it anymore," she said, continuing her search for the edge pieces. "There's nothing left to say."

"I disagree. Look, if you're flat-out not interested in me, fine. I can handle that. But if you're not willing to see where things might go with us because of some stupid rule—"

"It's not stupid. It's for our protection."

"I'm not going to hurt you or anyone else here. Why do you think I would? Why do you think anyone would?"

Because they had. Was it so hard to figure out? "I don't think you would hurt us, Ty. But if the rules are broken for me it would set a precedent and that can't happen because someone else might trust someone they shouldn't."

"Trust them with what?"

Holly tossed the puzzle piece onto the table and pinched the bridge of her nose. "Nothing. Things are just complicated. I told you that."

"Sweetheart, we passed complicated when you dragged me out of a plane."

Unable to respond to his statement she spied a certain piece and picked it up, setting it aside.

"What's that?" Ty shifted onto the floor beside her, too close, too *there*, for her to distance herself. Now would be a perfect time for Anna to make an appearance. A horribly, *perfect* time. "I always save it for last. It's my favorite," she said.

Ty leaned into her personal space to reach for the piece, giving it a thorough perusal. Alone, it was merely a dark piece of coated cardboard with a touch of yellow on the tip. But when it was placed with the others of its kind... It was the tunnel that led to the better beach, the bit of yellow sunlight guiding the way.

"Holly—"

"Rules are rules for a reason," she said by rote as she flipped over more pieces. "And on top of that I refuse to embarrass my family by breaking any more of our traditions than I already have. This is how we live, Ty. Dating you— It would never work."

"Holly, dear? Can you come give me a hand?" Anna called from the kitchen.

"Anna's making stew," she said, jumping at the excuse to get away from Ty. "She makes so much the pot is too heavy for her to lift. Coming, Anna!"

"I'll still be here when you get back," Ty said.

Holly stared down into his gorgeous eyes, memorizing every detail of his face. He'd still be there—for now. But not later.

Not when she faced the Elder Council and it mattered most.

CHAPTER EIGHT

The following morning Ty waited in the hallway for Anna to enter the kitchen before he quietly opened the front door of the house and left, limping along without his crutches. He held onto the railing as he descended the steps, and headed into the woods toward the path he remembered Holly taking from the village.

Anna would be upset if she discovered him gone but he wasn't going to listen to all the excuses he knew the woman would make if he told her his plans. He didn't want to hurt her feelings but the old gal had taken her duties as official sitter a little too seriously. He'd had enough coddling.

Now if the coddling came from Holly...

Holly had left for work this morning after feeding her dogs but he couldn't stand the thought of spending another day sitting on the couch in front of the television or with his nose in a book.

His foot was black and blue and sore as all get out but the swelling was down, and he was up for a little exploring. If not for the pass being closed and the trails too mangled to travel he'd be on his way back to Anchorage. Expending some energy and getting some exercise by checking out the village was definitely in order.

He picked his way along the trail, slipping twice and holding onto the trees for support. His ankle began to throb, but he kept going, refusing to turn back.

Spying the village from the trail, he saw that there were more people out today than when Holly had transported him from the infirmary on the sled. The lack of street lights or security lamps made visibility difficult and it suddenly struck him how dark the village actually was. He heard generators running but windows were covered, blocking out any illumination. To save heat? Or to not be noticed?

Moving into the village but sticking to the outer edges of the buildings, he saw a woman and two young children enter the general store, a little bell tinkling as the door opened and closed.

He liked checking out the little towns across Alaska. There were always hand-made novelties and crafts produced by the locals and he never knew what he might find. Gramps collected canes and pipes so Ty tried to find unusual designs to bring home.

Ty heard children singing inside the school as he passed, and on the far end of the street the smells of cinnamon and spices filled the air. He squinted in the dim light, able to make out lettering on a window. A bakery? Here? His stomach growled and he wondered if there was a place inside where he could sit down for a few minutes and take the weight off his foot.

Off to his left he spotted guards hurrying out of what Holly had referred to as the storage buildings. Unfortunately they saw him at the same time. Like they were looking for him? Anna must have sounded the alarm and informed someone that he'd left the house.

Ty felt their gazes zero in on him as he moved out of the shadows and because he was under such scrutiny he decided to duck into the general store.

Conversation stopped the moment he entered.

"Good morning," he said, dipping his head in a nod of greeting to both the mother he'd seen minutes earlier and the store's attendant.

"Good morning," the woman said softly, her eyes wide.

"Something I can help you find?" a sixty-something man asked from behind the counter. He wore an old-fashioned work apron over his clothes, and sucked on a pipe that wasn't lit.

"Just looking. Thought I might find a gift for my grandfather," he said, moving toward the items near the window. It, too, was covered but if he stood in just the right spot he was able to glimpse the outside.

Yeah, there. The guards stared in the direction of the store.

"Those were made by my wife," the store clerk said.

Ty glanced over his shoulder long enough to note that the woman and her children had moved to the back of the building. A rear exit? "They're nice," he said, only then looking down to see what it was the man was talking about.

Woven rugs. He saw one on top in various dark colors and grabbed it. "I'll take this one. Would you mind keeping it for me while I look around?"

"No problem at all. I'll wrap it up for you."

The man hurried off toward the counter and the old number-punch cash register while Ty shifted to the small selection of pipes displayed on a rack hanging in a narrow section of wall beside the window.

One of the guards talked on his radio, and both remained in front of the building making no attempt to disguise their interest.

Movement drew Ty's attention. Another man in camo left one of the storage buildings and hurried toward the store.

Ty pretended he didn't see the man's approach and grabbed a candle from another shelf. He lifted the jar and sniffed. Man, that was bad.

He replaced it and picked up another one in a different scent, counting the seconds until the bell jingled and a man's heavy-booted footsteps crossed the store's wood floor.

Pretending interest in his shopping, Ty sniffed and then drew back to look at the title. *Sugar Cookies.* Would Holly like that considering her penchant for sweets?

"Daddy!"

Ty glanced behind him and watched as the guard bent and brushed a quick kiss across the woman's cheek, whispering something to her in the process. The woman's gaze flicked toward Ty and then back to the man in front of her. A smile quickly appeared on her face. "We would love to meet you for lunch. How about we come back later," she said to the kids, "when Daddy's not around to see what we buy?"

"Not s'pose to see your presents before Christmas," the little girl said in a scolding tone.

The man in camo ruffled the girl's hair and agreed. "Go on, squirt. I'll be there as soon as I pick up a few things for the station."

The station. Now they had a police station?

In short order the mother ushered her children out of the store, leaving only Ty, the clerk and the guard— deputy?—behind.

Refusing to be rushed, Ty grabbed a vanilla scented candle to add to his purchases and moved on, aware that his every move was closely monitored.

Didn't they realize there was a fine line between being cautious and being paranoid?

Every stare, every weird thing that happened, upped his belief that this village was involved in something big.

He limped along the items in front of the window, trying to angle himself to get a better view despite the covering. When he found another spot, he lingered.

Two more camo-ed men had taken position across the street, doing a poor job of looking like it was a casual meet up for smokes.

The hair on the back of Ty's neck stood on end, the knot in his gut growing.

What was inside those buildings? How many guards or deputies or whatever title they went by did a little village need? Were they *actual* deputies? True law-enforcement or hired guns? And if so—hired for what?

Ty glanced down, still pretending to shop, and spotted a pretty cream-and-gray knitted hat he thought would look nice on Holly. He plucked it from the display, juggling the two candles in one arm. He couldn't stay here all day buying stuff just to watch the activity across the street. But maybe if the bakery had seating... What would happen if he left the store?

Deciding to find out, he turned and carried the items to the counter, adding a couple of gigantic suckers to the pile once he got there.

"Buying these for your family?"

"Yeah. Back in Anchorage."

"My grandchildren love those," the clerk said, ringing up the items with a deftness that defied the fact he had to carefully punch the old-time keys just so.

"I'm sure my niece and nephew will like them, too."

The guard shifted in Ty's peripheral vision, standing an aisle over.

Once Ty paid the total, he grabbed the bag in one hand and headed for the door but stopped just shy of the threshold. "I'm going to the bakery next," he said to the guard. "In case you or your buddies are interested."

The guard's jaw tightened and the clerk gave the younger man a nervous glance but neither of them commented.

Ty didn't stick around. He left the store, aware that still two more guards now stood shooting the breeze with the others outside of the storage buildings. If he had any remaining doubts they fizzled at the sight.

This wasn't a military base. Wasn't a town that needed that many deputies.

His mind raced with all the possible scenarios of what the buildings contained. Of what might be happening here.

Then came the realization that whatever it was, Holly's father was obviously involved.

No wonder Holly didn't want him asking questions.

CHAPTER NINE

Holly gasped when her office door burst open with no warning. "Devon, what on earth?"

"He's in the mercantile. I thought you said Anna was keeping an eye on him."

She didn't need to ask to whom Devon referred. "She is—was. How did he get there?"

"He walked."

She managed to restrain a groan, both at Ty's seeming determination to reinjure himself and Devon's visible anger. "I'll go get him."

"No. He'll be even more suspicious if you go running to retrieve him again like you did at the infirmary."

She refused to fight with him, especially now. "Devon, if you didn't want me to do something or go after Ty, why are you here?" she demanded, her frustration lending her words a harshness she didn't intend.

It would take time for things between her and Devon to level out. Time before he would be able to accept that they would never be what he wanted them to be.

Maybe she couldn't be with Ty but after kissing him, feeling the way she had after a few chaste kisses? She knew settling for less wasn't an option.

But in the meantime she and Devon had to be able to work together, closely together, without resorting to snipping at each other like peevish children.

"I do want you to do something. He has to be taken care of. Before the shipment arrives tomorrow."

"*What?*"

"Your father arranged it. It's already in flight. Apparently the first notification came while the transmitter was down but the second confirmation just arrived."

She dropped back down in the chair, her legs filled with jelly. Her mind scrambled for possible ways to distract Ty but blasting the stereo and keeping him inside the cottage wasn't going to drown out the sound of the cargo plane flying low over the village.

Devon pulled a small glass vial from his pocket and held it out to her.

"First thing tomorrow morning I want you to pour this in his drink. It will knock him out for about twelve hours."

She blinked at the white powder inside the glass. "Are you kidding me? No. Absolutely *not*." She couldn't comprehend... "Is that how you get rid of people who get too close to the village? You *drug them*?"

Holly stared into Devon's face, waiting for him to answer. Devon wasn't abusive, wasn't cold-hearted. Protective, yes. A pain in the butt sometimes, sure. But she found it hard to believe he would do such a thing.

Devon inhaled, his gaze narrowing on her even more than before. "Only as a last resort," he admitted.

Like that was a weakness?

"In case you haven't noticed, we're out of time. Holly, that shipment is coming tomorrow and we have to be ready to receive it, hide it and then move it. We can't take any chances and there's no way of guaranteeing he doesn't witness something he shouldn't except *this*. Take it. Use it. He'll sleep right through it."

Which would be best but— "No. I can't."

Ty might represent everything she had to protect the village from but she wasn't going to diminish his free will by unethical methods. "There's another way."

"How?"

Honestly? She didn't know. "I'll think of something. Something *else*."

Devon stretched out his arm and lowered the vial to her desk. "*That* is your something else. Use it, and I'll take care of the rest. Holly, this is your chance to right the wrong you created when you brought him here."

No. No, not like that. "Ty's still recovering from a head injury, and even if he wasn't—

Devon turned on his heel and stalked toward the door.

"Devon, wait." She jumped up from her chair to rush after him. She managed to get between him and the door, blocking his way. "I want us to be friends. Please? I can't bear the thought of never being able to talk to you again. Can't we go back to the way we were? Before you tried to be more and things got so crazy?"

He made a rough sound in his throat.

She placed her hand on his arm and felt the bunched muscles beneath his winter clothing. "That's not an answer."

Devon reached for the door and opened it, forcing her to step out of the way.

"I don't want to be your friend, Holly."

***

"I heard you got bored today," Holly said to Ty that evening after dinner.

When given the option of eating in the dining room or venturing into the kitchen, Ty had nearly groaned at the thought of taking the extra steps to the kitchen. He'd collapsed into one of the dining chairs, so tired he wondered if he'd make it through the meal without landing face-first in his plate.

His afternoon of adventuring had left his injured foot throbbing like someone poked hot steel rods into his heel and up his calf, but he wasn't about to let on that he'd overdone things. Or that he was even more suspicious of the activities in the village.

Now he sat on the floor in front of the couch, and split his attention between Holly and Anna and the puzzle he was supposed to be completing.

He had to be wrong. His background in the military made him suspicious of any subversive activity and now his imagination had taken over.

But how many times had he learned the most dangerous warriors were the women fighting for their cause? How many times had a bomb-strapped female approached a sentry post just so she could take out the soldiers guarding it and die a martyr?

Were they militia? Mob? Was Holly some kind of mafia princess?

Russian mafia?

It might sound crazy but it wasn't... Not entirely.

He owed it to Gramps and Beth's kids to get home in one piece but he owed it to his country, his brothers-in-arms, to get to the bottom of whatever was happening here.

And to appease your curiosity about a certain blond?

"Can I have that piece? I know where it goes," Holly said.

Realizing he held the puzzle shape she wanted, Ty handed it over without comment.

A fire blazed in the living room hearth, easing the chill in the room. Anna sat in the rocker closest to the fire, knitting as fast as her fingers could move, and Holly sat opposite him, the blaze behind her giving her hair a golden glow.

"Did you find anything you liked at the mercantile?" Holly asked.

"A few things, yeah." He leaned back against the couch cushions, the coffee table between them and the half-completed puzzle atop it. They might accomplish more if he could stop staring at Holly and wondering if she was a traitor to everything he held dear.

"I could have made arrangements to take you after I got home from work, you know. We could have used the snowmobiles."

"I needed some air. There is only so much television a guy can watch." He forced himself to scan the puzzle's edge for the right match, hoping to stumble across one.

"Well, since you're obviously up for it, I was wondering if you'd like to spend the day with me tomorrow? The dogs need a run, and I could use a break from the office."

He fit a piece into place and tried to act casual but his synapses were firing faster than he could sort through them. For someone who wanted to keep him out of the village and off his foot, why so accommodating all of a sudden? "You don't have to work?"

"I'm mostly caught up. And the weather is supposed to be mild for this area and time of year. Usually that means another storm is on its way. I thought since you're almost healed and so ready to get home we might make that trip to see *Nessie*."

His suspicions grew by leaps and bounds. As did his disappointment. He could overlook and forgive a lot of things but not deception. Not on any level. His mother had lied to his father for months about her affairs. Lied to him and Beth about where she was going and why they had to stay alone. Why she was leaving them. "That's a really nice offer."

"I thought you would enjoy it. It would allow you to get out of the house for a while *but* still keep you off your foot," she said. "Does it hurt after your walk?"

He almost did the typical guy thing and denied the pain before he caught himself. Let them—Holly and the sheriff and whoever else was involved here—think what they like. The element of surprise might be needed later. "I wasn't going to say anything but, yeah. I may have overdone it a bit. I'd love to go sledding, though. When do we leave?"

He knew now where the phrase 'killer smile' came from. If Holly was involved in something as serious as he believed given their location so close to Russia or the Soviet Union or whatever they were calling themselves now, she was *good*.

Beautifully, wonderfully, intriguingly good—at lying.

"Early. Say seven?"

He picked up another puzzle piece and spotted the correct placement right away. Too bad he couldn't get such an easy read on Holly.

Guilty or innocent? Victim—or active participant?

"I have a surprise for you, too."

He glanced up, watching the play of firelight on her features. "Oh?"

"I thought we could stop by my cave. There's a hot spring, so you could soak your foot and ease the pain that's making you frown so hard."

Innocent until proven guilty, he reminded himself.

"The cave?" Anna asked, her surprise evident. "You're taking him there?"

Holly fitted a piece of the puzzle into place, taking more time than was necessary. Avoiding her aunt?

"It will help his foot, Anna. We have to make sure Ty is as fit as he can be for the trek home, right?"

"Yes… I suppose," Anna said, her tone sounding more than a bit worried.

Ty wondered if Holly's offer had ulterior motives but he'd be lying if he said he wasn't tempted by the idea. Maybe alone, away from everyone else, she would open up more about what was going on? Shed some light on the situation? It sounded like an awesome way to spend the day.

Which pretty much guarantees she's taking you for a different sort of ride and the hot spring and Nessie are the lures.

Disappointment filled him once more. He grabbed another puzzle piece and wondered if the knot in his gut was the same feeling animals felt when their master tricked them into the car with the promise of a treat.

Isolated rides into the woods never ended well.

He had no reason to believe his would be different.

***

"You'll be careful?" Anna asked for the dozenth time the next morning.

"Yes." Holly finished packing a lunch for Ty and herself and zipped the flexible cooler closed, placing it with the other items she was taking with her on the ride.

She looked up and found Anna watching, her face pinched. "Anna, stop worrying. I told you why I have to do it this way."

"Yes, yes," Anna agreed, her voice hushed, "Devon's method isn't at all acceptable but you should take someone else *with* you."

"I'll be fine."

"I suppose I could go along."

"You would be cold and miserable."

"At one point I loved to travel but my old bones ache bouncing around on that sled. Oh, what will your mama and papa think of me, letting you hie off alone with him?"

Anna folded her wrinkled hands in front of her and wrung them like a washcloth. Combined with her blue-and-green flannel nightgown and robe, with thick socks and the suede slippers Holly had given her for her birthday last month, she looked decidedly fragile. No, Anna didn't need to be out in the cold.

"They'll think you know me well enough to know I can handle myself. Please, stop worrying." Holly wrapped her arm around Anna's shoulders and squeezed, giving the older woman a kiss on the cheek. "We'll be back later."

"What if things are...delayed? If there's a problem?"

"Then we'll spend the night at the cave."

"Alone?" Anna tsked. "It's not proper. What will the village think? He's a handsome man who is no longer injured or feeble."

"The village will think what they like regardless of what I do or don't do. Anna, I can handle this. Besides, we've spent enough time with Ty to know he isn't a man who would force himself on a woman."

"That's true. If he wasn't an outsider, he would be quite a catch for a girl your age. And with babies, too. A man with babies needs a woman in his life."

Not what she wanted to hear. She had enough on her mind already, without adding Ty or the children in his care to the mix.

Ty had shared photos of his niece and nephew. A little boy with curly hair and a shy grin, and the little girl... Oh, she was beautiful. Impish.

But Ty *was* an outsider, even though she didn't think of him as an outsider anymore. To her he was just a man. A good, hardworking, caring, perfectly flawed man who loved his family and appealed to her because of it.

Careful there.

Her emotions were edging into deeper waters she wasn't sure she could tread. Her feelings had to be the result of their close quarters, the curiosity and intrigue of meeting a new person, someone different from those around her. Her feelings for Ty weren't special. How could they be when he didn't know her? Not the *real* her.

The urge to tell him the truth was so strong sometimes that she had to physically draw away from him, move out of the room, force herself to think of the consequences, just to stay strong.

Other women in their village might have the option of choosing Ty, of turning their backs on the village and the sacred mission, but not her. The future leader of their group could *not* be with one of *them*.

"We ready to go?" Ty asked as he nudged his way through the swinging door.

Holly grabbed the second cooler full of fresh water for the dogs and slid the strap over her shoulder, forcing her impossible dreams back into the recesses of her mind.

"When you are." Ty looked big and handsome but tired despite turning in early last night. After working on the puzzle for a while they had retreated to their separate bedrooms in preparation of today.

Ty shouldn't be doing anything today except sitting on the couch recovering but that wasn't possible. His adventure to the mercantile had cost him and throughout last night's dinner she had noticed every grimace and frown that accompanied the white line of pain around his mouth. He wasn't up to this trip but she had to get him underground before the first cargo plane appeared.

"All of that goes?" Ty asked, lifting a hand to point at the supplies she had stacked by the door.

"Your body burns a lot of energy trying to stay warm. We'll need to snack throughout the day."

Ty moved close. Close enough for her to get a sniff of his cologne and see the little crinkles at the corners of his green eyes. He was attractive, no doubt about it, but there was something else about him that… made her wish for the impossible.

"Any of Anna's oatmeal cookies in there?"

As though she could go a day without them? Holly smiled and shoved her thoughts away once more. "Of course. I even snagged a few extra."

In minutes they were loaded up and out the door. The dogs were harnessed and waiting, loud in their excitement.

Ty sent her a look of classic male frustration when he had to sit in the basket of the sleigh rather than take the position of control.

Maybe she would let him take a practice run with the sled in the clearing. If there was time and he felt up to it.

Anna had asked for pine to begin decorating for Christmas and because it would take several trips to gather enough, Holly had included a limb-cutter and a drag-sack for their trip as well.

Holly said one last goodbye to Anna and got the team going, taking a trail in the opposite direction of where they were headed.

She had to disorient Ty by taking false trails so he wouldn't be able to find the village later. It would double their time in the cold and mean some rough terrain given the downed limbs but she knew it would be worth it in the end. After all, better safe than sorry.

And considering she had gone against Devon's plan and she was alone with Ty, responsible for keeping him safe as well as the flight-drop a secret, sorry was the last thing she wanted to be.

CHAPTER TEN

Ty settled back in the sled, warm beneath the blankets protecting him from the ice and snow kicked up by the dogs' pace. When they left the cottage they had headed east, then south, then north and finally veered east again before turning west and then south once more.

Ty didn't say anything or ask why Holly was making circles because he knew the answer. Everything she did was to protect the village and whatever was going on there. It didn't take a genius to figure out all the wandering around on the brushy, bumpy trails was Holly's attempt to confuse him.

It would have worked—except for the fact he had a keen sense of direction and despite all of the twists and turns and loops Holly made, Ty knew the village was about twelve miles northeast from where they now were. He didn't need a GPS to tell him that. His internal guidance system had saved his butt more than once during tricky maneuvers.

Finally they left the woods and entered a clearing that stretched long and white in front of them. Ty searched for signs of *Nessie* but didn't see the plane anywhere. Was this the right spot?

The Brooks Mountain Range was seven hundred miles long. Who knew how many small valleys there were? Plus finding the plane via the light of the moon was like that whole needle in a haystack scenario.

As Holly directed the sled team into a clearing, the crash came back to him. He remembered spotting a patch of white amongst the green forest below him. That spot had to be this clearing—approximately eight miles from her village, he mused, making a mental map.

"See it yet?" Holly asked, calling the words over the noise of the rails sliding over the ice-crusted snow.

He shook his head, searching... Finally something began to take shape up in the darkness ahead of them and he realized it was the tail end of the Cessna. The wind was at their backs, blowing toward the tree line in front of them. *Nessie* was buried in snow up to her wings and nose—or at least what was left of her.

Holly slowed the dogs and guided them as close as possible to the wreckage. The up-close view of the plane smashed into the pines brought a tightness to his chest he couldn't ignore. He'd been in that. Might still be in it if Holly hadn't answered his distress call.

The front of the Cessna was smashed, the cockpit exposed, snow piled high in the pilot's seat. Had Holly not arrived that night he would have died here, in this spot. Under that snow. Instead, he'd been granted the miracle he'd prayed for.

Which brought up the question—if something *was* going on inside the village, if Holly's family was a part of some sort of illicit network, was he going to turn his back on the people—the person—who had helped him? Rescued him? What if the good guys were bad guys too?

"Ty? You okay?"

He struggled to get out of the sleigh, stiff from sitting so long while Holly tried to disorient him. He left his crutches behind and hobbled to the aircraft to take a closer look. "You climbed inside here?"

"You don't remember climbing out?"

He did. Some. The details were more than a little vague.

"You were so calm," Holly said from behind him. "It was probably shock but I appreciated it because I was freaking out enough for both of us. And can I say now that when you had to stop and yank your foot out from under the instrument panel my heart just about *stopped*? I was so afraid your foot wouldn't be attached and blood was going to gush and I wouldn't be able to save you."

Surviving this was more than luck. How many could have made it out with only bruises and a concussion to show for it?

Suddenly, he didn't care what she was involved in. Whatever it was appeared to be family-based. She'd been born into it rather than given a choice. That mattered, right?

How could he hold her responsible when she had been willing to sacrifice herself to help him the way she had? And then she'd taken him home, ticking off everyone in her village from the appearance of things.

He had reason to be suspicious of Holly and the others in the village but here on this spot all he could be was thankful. If he did anything, he had to help Holly find a way out, find a way to protect her. "Come here," he ordered softly, sitting in the gaping hull with his feet sprawled outside on the mounded snow.

Holly moved closer to him, taking his outstretched hand, her gaze soft and full of understanding.

Once she was in front of him he took off his gloves and palmed her face, stroking his thumbs over her silky skin. "Thank you."

What was it about her? What made him want to hold her? Be with her, no matter what? Not casually but—from now on? He barely knew her. *Didn't* know her.

As though sensing his thoughts and intent to kiss her, Holly pulled away, her breath blowing white in the air.

"You're welcome," she said, not quite looking at him.

He had to be wrong about things. About her. Had. To. Be.

"Although Anna's right. You *are* a flirt," she said, her head tilted to one side as she regarded him with a sad-looking smile.

"Only with you." Holly's laughter rang out, surrounding him, warming him. "Hey, I mean it. Every word."

The breeze blew her hair into her face and she tried to nudge it back with her glove. Ty reached out and helped her, tucking it beneath her thick knit cap.

"Thanks."

"Any time."

"Okay, so...here," she said, awkwardly pulling a disposable camera out of her coat pocket. "This is for you. Why don't you take the pictures you want and we'll get moving?"

"Sounds good."

"We, um, have to cross the valley to get to the cave... Wanna try your hand at mushing? If you're foot is up to it, that is."

He looked at her in surprise. She was going to hand over her team to him? "Seriously?"

"Considering all the grumbling looks you send me when you have to ride in the basket, do you think I'd kid you about something like that?"

"No. I just thought you'd never ask."

***

"Whoa!" Holly was insanely nervous by the time she pulled the dogs to a stop outside the gate leading to her sanctuary.

Ty's near-kiss back at the plane had scattered her senses, and seeing him handle the sled team with such ease had her admiring his patience and skill.

The long trek to the cave gave her plenty of time to think. Plenty of time to realize that no matter what the future had in store, no matter when Ty left, he would take a piece of her heart with him. "Stay there."

She set the snow hook and hopped of the rails of the sled, opening the gate to the cave's entry. She was an animal lover but long ago one of her great-grandfathers had insisted the protection be installed, unwilling to risk his wife or child from stumbling upon a hibernating bear or wolf seeking shelter there as well.

In minutes the dogs and Ty were inside the gate, the sled sliding easily on the exposed, snow-packed cave floor. The team eagerly pulled them deeper into the recesses of the mountain, until the snow and ice was too thin for the sled to travel on. They had to go the rest of the way on foot. "Good job, guys. Moxie, well done."

"This is amazing," Ty said, his voice bouncing off the rock walls.

Yes, it was. But now that she was here with him she wondered at the wisdom of her decision.

Would she ever be able to come here again and *not* think of him? Remember this brief period of time and the man who— made her want more?

The knot in her stomach grew. This was the last time she would able to spend time alone with Ty. Soon the trails through the pass would be cleared enough to travel and given Ty's determination and strength, he would be able to hike where necessary.

Ty looked around the first chamber while she took a few minutes to care for the dogs. Once the animals were taken care of she handed Ty a lantern. "This way," she said as she grabbed the coolers and moved into the deepest part of the cave. He tried to do the gentlemanly thing and take several of the bags from her but she clutched them tighter. "With your injury, you'll need a hand free to keep your balance. Carry the flashlight. I've got these."

The bubbling hot water spring brought a sense of peace to Holly as she followed Ty into her private oasis.

"Unbelievable," he said, his tone filled with awe. "How did you find this place?"

"I didn't. It was handed down to me."

"It's some inheritance."

"It is, isn't it? My great-great-grandfather discovered it and my family has used it ever since as our private hideaway. Stay there," she ordered, removing herself from his side.

She dropped the coolers and bags she carried long enough to light several oil lanterns and the cave immediately brightened with a warm yellow glow. In a matter of minutes she lit several more located around the cave and turned to face her first ever guest.

"Canned goods, kindling, bottled water. Enough food to last several weeks. Sleeping bags, pillows, medical supplies. Anything you don't have in here?"

"A, um, maid," she said, scrambling to pick up a few of the clothes she'd scattered the last time she'd been there and left in such a hurry.

Ty whistled, the sound long and low.

"I see you've spotted my guilty pleasure."

"I can definitely see why you don't share." He turned to face her. "Sure you don't mind?"

Surprisingly, she didn't mind at all. Even though she had never brought anyone here, especially not a man, as she stood there and watched Ty limp painfully toward the pool she realized how badly she wanted this quiet alone-time with him. How much she wanted this memory.

Yes, he would leave. Yes, he *had* to leave. But right now? Right here? "I don't mind at all. Make yourself comfortable. I know your ankle and foot are hurting."

"They are some," he admitted, the words rueful. "But I loved racing over that clearing. I needed to burn some energy."

Ty stripped off his coat, shoes, and outer layers before limping toward the pool. His socks were last and his sigh of relief echoed off the cavern walls after he rolled up his pant legs and stuck his feet into the bubbly depths.

Holly discreetly grabbed a few more items from the floor and removed her coat and layers as well. That done, she carried the coolers to the pool and sat down a few feet from him.

"Ow."

"Something wrong?"

"I'm sitting on a rock." He pulled it out from beneath his upper thigh and held it up with two fingers.

Holly took it and ran her thumb over the streak in the surface. "Lucky you."

"Why's that?"

She handed it back to him. "This place is so special I guess I think the rocks are, too. Consider it a gift from me to you. To remember our special day."

Ty tossed the rock into the air once, catching it and tucking it into the pocket of his jeans.

"The food smells good."

Holly blinked at the comment and sudden change in topic. "Is that your way of saying you're hungry?"

"Well, I didn't want to be rude. You just gave me a memory rock."

She laughed at the way his mind worked and handed him a wrapped sandwich. Typical man.

After eating their lunch and bickering about things like who was going to get the last cookie and who would be the one to place the most puzzle pieces tonight when they returned to the cottage, Holly scooped her hand into the water and splashed Ty.

His expression was priceless.

Surprise. Debate. Then attack.

Holly shrieked as Ty grabbed hold of her and wrestled her down beside him, pinning her arms with his body and dipping his hand into the pool. "No!" she said, barely able to get the word out because she was laughing so hard.

He was so strong. His green eyes sparkled with teasing intent as he leaned over her.

"Paybacks, sweetheart."

"I'll melt," she said, breathless. "I'm too sweet!"

Ty's chest moved against her as he chuckled. "It's all those cookies you eat. But, still—payback. Or I could just toss you in completely."

"Nooooooo! Don't!" she cried when he pretended to follow through on his threat. "I'll freeze on the way home. Splash me."

A predatory gleam entered his eyes. "No, I don't think so. That's too easy."

Too easy? "You were going to a second ago!"

"Changed my mind. But I might be persuaded to consider letting you go."

"Oh, really?" she asked, happy to see the tension Ty had carried all morning long disappearing with their play. She liked this side of him. Playful, fun, without his worries weighing on him. "What's the price?"

"A kiss, freely given."

Well, it wasn't quite free when it was a ransom but she wasn't going to argue a technicality.

One last kiss?

Relaxing beneath him she smiled her willingness to hand over such a harsh punishment but he didn't move.

She tugged her hands free from between them and slid them around his neck to pull him low. His fingers touched her face, the tips calloused but gentle, warm from the water.

Their lips met and she tightened her arms around his neck to increase the pressure of the kiss. Sitting on the rock ledge with their feet in the pool, Holly could barely open her eyes by the time it ended.

"Sweetheart..."

She nodded but then quickly shook her head, blinking. "I should check on the dogs," she said, swinging her legs out of the pool and moving away from him as quickly as she could given her feet slipped on the rock floor. "Take your time."

Ty stared up at her, the look in his eyes making her think he was as confused by things as she was.

"Holly...?"

Ty knew enough about her home and the village to know their time together was limited. She couldn't give him more.

***

Something disturbed Ty, and he frowned when he realized he wasn't home in Anchorage with the kids and Gramps, but somewhere warm and...*bubbling?*

He opened his eyes and stared up at the cave ceiling, only then remembering he'd gotten out of the pool and walked around Holly's hideaway to check it out before lowering himself onto the couch to wait for Holly's return.

He sat up, the light from the lanterns allowing him to spot Holly curled up sound asleep on the bed across the room.

His stare lingered on her, the softness of her face, the way her hair flowed over the pillow beneath her cheek.

The dogs barked and whined in the other chamber and he realized that's what had disturbed him. He frowned at the noise, wondering how Holly was able to sleep through it. But then she spent so much time with her animals she was no doubt used to the noise.

Staring at her while she slept, he noted the faint shadows under her eyes and remembered the long hours she worked.

Afraid the ruckus would wake her, he decided to check on the dogs himself. It was probably an animal sniffing around the gate. This deep into the mountain range anything was possible.

Ty left the comfort of the couch. The large, thick rugs covering the cave floor muffled his footsteps across the cavern to the carved stone steps leading back to the first chamber. The dogs were gone, the noise they made echoing off the cave walls from the mountain entrance. He used the wall for balance, paying care to not reinjure his ankle on the icy cavern floor. "Hey, what's going on?"

Several of the dogs paced nervously in front of the gate but Moxie approached Ty and pressed her head to his thigh to be petted. "Yeah, girl. What's up, huh?"

A few whines, a bark or two. Lots of pacing. The dogs pressed their muzzles between the bars of the gates, shaking with their excitement, but Ty didn't see anything on the other side. "Come on, stop. Whatever it is, they can't get us in here."

The dogs didn't care.

Ty dimmed the lantern and set it aside, giving his eyes time to adjust. He still didn't see anything.

At first. "What—"

Something fell from the sky, rocking back and forth in the wind.

Ty squinted and hugged his arms around himself to battle the cold, watching. Yeah, he wasn't imagining that.

It was dark, the cloud-spotted sky lit only by the moon so it was hard to make out details, but— Was that a parachute?

Two parachutes.

Three.

Four.

Five.

He searched the sky, finally able to discern the low rumble of powerful engines between bouts of barking and whines.

A drop was taking place even though Holly had said the village was ninety-nine percent self-sufficient. Had she lied to him or was this the one percent she hadn't told him about?

The plane flew low, beneath radar range. And then, as he stood there and stared despite the bitter cold, a second plane appeared and dropped even *more* crates. Why so many of them?

The planes kept coming, making their drops.

And then he knew the real reason Holly had brought him to her special hideaway. The awareness punched him in the gut and stripped him of any remaining illusions.

Holly was definitely one of them.

***

Holly opened her eyes when she heard Ty swear.

She sat up, groggy and disoriented. In all the time he'd been there, she'd never heard him curse. "Ty?"

"No supply flights?" he asked simply, limping deeper into the inner chamber.

The moment she saw his face she knew whatever she said wouldn't matter. His expression was stamped with fury, his motions jerky as he yanked on his discarded outer layers.

Going with the only thing she could think of under such pressure she said,

"None that land. Did you hurt yourself? Your ankle?"

"Don't change the subject. What are they dropping?"

Ty glared at her and she struggled to maintain eye contact.

"What's in those crates, Holly?"

Every fear, every doubt, every reminder of the horrors of what could go wrong filled her head. "Supplies."

"So that's the way it is, huh? Answer me something else then. Truthfully. Did you bring me here just to keep me from seeing the drop? So I wouldn't be in the village when it arrived?"

She hated the accusation in his tone. Hated the way he looked at her. Hated the truth. "I thought you would enjoy it a-and it would help your ankle heal."

"And because we're underground, you didn't think I'd hear them," he added. "Too bad you didn't think about the dogs barking."

She cringed. How could she have forgotten about the dogs? They always barked and made a fuss when the planes flew over because the noise was so rare. "Ty—"

"What does your family think about you sharing such an intimate location with me— the *outsider*? Better yet, what does Barney think?"

"Ty, they're just supplies."

"Like I'm going to believe anything you say after you've lied *how* many times?"

"I haven't lied to you. I just haven't—"

"Told me the truth? You brought me here to hide the drop. Say it."

"Okay! I did! But— That's not the *only* reason." How could he think that of her?

"If it's just supplies, what's the big secret?"

She shoved her hair off her face, her mind struggling to find the words. "Because of the stunt you pulled yesterday."

Ty moved close to her, his coat dangling from his hand. "What stunt did I pull? I walked into the village. I bought gifts for my family from a store. How is that a stunt?"

Oh, she was making a mess of this. "I told you how the villagers feel about outsiders. If you wanted to go to the mercantile, why didn't you wait until Anna or I could go with you? Or was that the point *you* had to make?"

She watched as his expression tightened and knew she was right. He was suspicious of the compound's purpose—which meant she had all the more reason to be cautious. "Ty, any goodwill you may have made by being a nice guy was undone the moment you snuck out of the house. Do you have any idea how upset Devon was because you kept staring at the supply buildings?"

"I was shopping."

"You were investigating the storage buildings and the village," she said.

Ty gripped the thick coat in both hands and squeezed.

"If those buildings are used for nothing but storage take me through them. *Show* me. Bring Devon and some of his guards along so they can tackle me if I touch something, but prove you're telling the truth, Holly."

"Why should I have to *prove* anything?'" she asked, her hands shaking as she yanked and pulled and tugged her weather gear into place. The peace and pleasantness of the day was over. There was no going back from here.

"Are you running drugs through the village?"

Drugs? "No."

"Guns?"

"No!"

"Russian illegals? Nuclear weaponry? *What?*"

She swung to face him, shaking her head. "Ty, you're just going to have to trust me when I say it's nothing like that. Please, believe me."

"Why should I believe you when you can't tell me the truth? Trust runs both ways, sweetheart."

That it did. And even though she wanted to confide in him, she couldn't. Not with so much at stake.

Ty stared at her, his expression angry and filled with disappointment. "What could possibly warrant that much devotion and loyalty from you but not be illegal?" He pressed both palms to his face and rubbed hard, ending the move with a punch to the air. "What are you involved in? Holly, tell me and maybe I can help you. I can take you to the police—the real police, not the one back there pretending to be."

As Holly stared at him her mind began to go numb, unable to comprehend the many questions and demands he flung at her in his anger.

Why hadn't she listened to Devon and Anna? Let Devon handle things as he'd done in the past? She wouldn't change the events that saved Ty's life but the ones after he was out of danger? The moments that now led to her feeling as though she was being slowly ripped apart? Those were the moments she would redo, the ones that would ease the harsh, twisted wad of emotions churning inside her. "It's not bad," she whispered, knowing he didn't believe her but needing to say it anyway. "I just can't tell you."

Holly stared at him, her hands fisted at her sides like that would keep the pain from spilling out, so that she wouldn't reveal more of her feelings for Ty than she already had.

"Take me back to the cottage," he said. "I want to get my belongings and then I want you to take me wherever it is I have to go to get out of here."

She couldn't let things end like this. Not with him hating her. "Ty, please—"

"No. Whatever it is you're involved in, Holly? I want no part of it."

CHAPTER ELEVEN

Ty's mood didn't improve when Holly went out of her way to make sure the ride back to the village lasted even longer than the one to the crash site and cave. He didn't think there was a single trail left to travel, and with every bumpy, deceptive turn his anger grew.

But it made him angrier still when he realized Holly had taken a roundabout route to the house, bypassing the village and the so-called storage buildings entirely. Like that mattered now? With the men and artillery guarding the place, he wouldn't make it far if he tried to sneak in. The trip to the mercantile was proof of that.

When they arrived at the cottage, Ty got off the sleigh and limped up the steps. He entered the house and immediately headed down the hall toward his bedroom. He didn't care if he had to sleep on the floor of a hangar or in a kennel like Holly's, he couldn't stay there.

There was no reason to hide mere supplies. Gas, fuel, grain. Water. Protect them? Yes. Guard them? Sure. But hide them? No. Whatever had dropped out of the sky this afternoon was big and abundant and Holly had gone beyond the call of duty to keep him from seeing it, even though the plan had failed.

Crazier still was that he felt so much for a woman he barely knew, much less for someone seemingly bent on self-destruction. He wasn't going to wait around to find out what her little off-the-grid community had up its sleeve. That was something for the authorities to investigate.

He grabbed his duffles from the floor and quickly packed the couple changes of clothing stored away in drawers, adding the presents he'd bought for Gramps and the kids. But then he remembered the candle he'd purchased for Holly and stupid as it sounded, he pulled it from the bag and left it on the dresser along with the knitted hat, and the ruffled apron he'd picked up for Anna.

"Leaving those behind?"

He didn't turn to face Holly. He used the excuse of battling the zipper and bulk, taking his anger out on the objects. "The apron is for Anna. The rest are for you. To say thanks for taking care of me."

"Oh… Ty—"

"Where's my gun?"

"Devon has it."

Was Holly going to be able to get him out of the village without the sheriff's interference? If she repeated the questions he'd asked at the cave to the good "sheriff", Ty would bet the gun might come in handy. "Let's go."

"Not tonight. The dogs are tired."

He zipped the second duffle closed and lifted it onto his shoulder, the other in his hand. "I'll find another team then."

Ty walked to the door but Holly stood in the way. She didn't budge at his approach and despite his anger he had to give her props for standing her ground.

"Ty, please. Can't you believe me? Because you believe *in* me? I'm telling you the truth," she whispered. "Those drops were just supplies."

"Then let me see them."

"I can't—but we're not what you think."

"Why should I believe that?" he demanded. "I walk down the street and guards follow me. I'm not allowed to enter a *supply building* because it's top secret. It makes no sense. Give me a reason. Give me something, Holly."

"I gave you something," she whispered. "My cave. I don't take people there. I've *never* taken anyone there. It's mine but you— I took *you*. I let—"

"You took him *where*?" Devon growled from the end of the hall.

Ty watched as the man shoved the coffee mug he carried in Anna's direction and stalked toward them.

"Devon, stop it. Ty didn't— Stop and listen to me. That's an *order*!" Holly said, raising her voice.

Ty dropped the duffles and widened his stance, ready and more than willing for whatever the good sheriff was about to dish out. "An order?" he repeated, zeroing in on the word. "Now that's interesting. Why are you taking orders from her, *sheriff?*"

Holly positioned herself between them.

"Ty wants to leave. I'm sledding him out tomorrow morning, as soon as the dogs are rested," Holly said.

"Why are you taking orders from her?" Ty repeated, staring into the man's rock-hard gaze and ignoring the gentle press of Holly's back against his chest. In another life, another time, another town, he could've fallen for her.

Ah, who are you kidding?

Devon glanced down at Holly. "Move."

"Devon, don—"

Devon reached out, picked Holly up and put her in the hall like a sack of potatoes.

"You like her," Ty said to Devon, seeing the man's gentleness towards Holly despite his anger. "Maybe you feel more for her. So how can you sit back and let her endanger herself? You think you can protect her when the officials close in? Because they will eventually. You can't make drops like the one I saw today and get by with it for long."

"Our supplies are nothing the officials need to be concerned with," Devon stated.

"What are you running through here? Because either Holly is a really good liar when she says it's not illegal or—"

Devon's fist plowed into Ty's jaw, hard and fast and appearing out of nowhere. Stars circled his eyes like in the cartoons.

"Devon, what are you *doing*!" Holly cried.

"My job."

Ty stumbled backward, his knees buckling when the room tilted. He tried to shake off the haze but hit the floor, his head spinning from the sucker punch.

Something sharp pricked his skin and he turned his head in time to see a hypodermic. They were drugging him? That wasn't playing fair.

The room shifted and moved above his head like some sort of out-of-body merry-go-round. Holly's face appeared in front of his, her lips mouthing words he couldn't hear due to the tunnel he'd fallen into. He blinked, tried to focus.

What was she saying?

Someone pushed Holly out of the way and grabbed hold of his wrist. He felt himself being yanked upright, over, until all he could see was camo pants and back of black combat boots.

Then…nothing at all.

***

"There you are."

Ty didn't look up at his grandfather as the man entered the garage. "Dishes done?"

"Yeah. I came out here to warn you Abbie learned a new word. She opened the door on me when I was in the john."

Ty chuckled at the news, tightening the bolt on the bike. "Do I wanna know what the word was?"

"Probably not. If anyone asks just tell'em she picked it up from television. It's said on there enough, that's for sure. Ain't nothing good on TV no more."

Gramps walked over and looked at Ty's untouched plate. "Too well done for you?"

"No, it was fine. Just wasn't hungry."

"You haven't eaten or said much since you got home. Now you're out here putting Logan's bike together? It couldn't wait?"

"I've been gone two weeks. I've fallen behind on the chores."

"Son, you obviously couldn't talk in front of the kids when you got here but don't think you're not going to tell me what happened out there. Where have you been? Where did you stay before you wound up in Bettles?"

Ty's inner arm pulsed in response to Gramps' question. The exact spot where the needle had been inserted to finish the job of knocking him out. "I'm not sure. Some off-the-grid village. I don't know the name of it." Because no one had ever called it by name. Not Holly, not Anna. He couldn't even remember seeing a name on the store window or the schoolhouse or the bakery.

There were times in the past few days when he wondered if he had dreamt it all. He'd opened his eyes in a doctor's home practice in Bettles, and according to the doc a man had found him dazed, bleeding and hypothermic in the woods where the man was hunting. That Ty had repeatedly said he'd crashed his plane.

The only problem with that was that he hadn't been anywhere near Bettles when he'd gone down.

Of course the good Samaritan who had brought him to the doc's house had disappeared without leaving a name, too. Ty guessed it was another one of the sheriff's tricks for getting rid of unwanted guests. "Gramps, I called you, right?"

The old man frowned at him. "Several days after I got an email from someone saying you were safe, yes."

"Do you still have it? The email?" Maybe he could have an IT buddy trace the web address.

"Should be on the computer."

Ty left the bike behind to finish later and headed into the house. The computer was in the living room.

"What's this about?" Gramps asked, following.

Ty clicked to retrieve the email and scanned both new and old.

"That's weird. I didn't delete it."

But it was gone all the same.

"Those crazy machines can't be trusted," Gramps mumbled.

No, it was the people behind the message that couldn't be trusted. "What about the phone call? What did I say?"

"I only caught a few words here and there," Gramps said, scratching his nose. "There was lots of static but you said you were safe, and would be home soon. Ty, you feelin' all right? Are you sure that knot on your head isn't more serious?"

Ty ignored the question. "When did I call you? That was before the doctor in Bettles called, right?"

Gramps laid his hand on Ty's shoulder and squeezed. "Son, what's going on? What happened while you were gone?"

"Nothing." Maybe he *had* been so out of it that he'd dreamt it all. Dreamed of the hidden, snowy village and Holly and Anna's home cooking. Maybe after the crash he'd wandered around in the snow and hallucinated his rescuing angel? Was that possible?

He rubbed his hand over his tired, gritty eyes and along his jaw, wincing when the move put pressure on the bruise purpling his jaw up like a pickled egg. He hadn't dreamt getting sucker punched by the so-called sheriff. He had the multi-colored skin to show for it and the teeth-ravaged inner jaw shredded to bits thanks to the blow.

But the bruise could also be explained by the crash. Or a fall when he was staggering through the snow?

He had nothing to show for his time in the village. The gifts he'd purchased for Gramps and the kids from the little village where he couriered supplies, his gun, his clothes. Everything *except* the items he'd bought at the mercantile in Holly's village.

The two twenties he'd paid the store clerk were tucked inside the leather wallet with the rest of his money. *Like it had never happened.* Except—

"Where you going?" Gramps called as Ty jumped from the chair and raised up the stairs three at a time.

"Ty? What's going on?"

Ty ignored his grandfather's huffing and puffing presence when the old man finally made it to Ty's bedroom. He was too busy trying to find the clothes he'd worn home. He dug through the pile of dirty laundry on the floor and found his jeans. What pocket was it in? Had they stripped him of the rock Holly had given him, too?

"Ty? Son, you've gotta fill me in on what you are looking for."

Ty's fingers closed over the rock and he pulled it from the denim, holding it in his fist like a talisman. "Yes! You thought you had me, didn't you, sheriff?"

"Sheriff? You're in trouble with the law?"

Ty punched the air, the rock in his hand, and grabbed Gramps by the shoulders, hugging him.

He wasn't crazy. He hadn't dreamt up a really elaborate story in his head about Holly and Anna and the mercantile. This was his rock. His gift from Holly. Proof his memory was intact.

"What is it? Let me see," Gramps ordered.

Ty opened his hand and let Gramps take it.

His adrenaline was pumping now. Holly and the crash, the whole scenario. They weren't a cold-induced dream.

"You gave me a heart attack climbing those stairs to see— Hooooo, son, where did you get this?"

"Someone gave it to me."

"Gave it to you? Somebody *gave* this to you? Do you know what this is?"

"It's a memory rock," he said, quoting Holly.

"I'd say," Gramps agreed. "A pretty valuable one too."

"What do you mean?"

Gramps held the rock up between his thumb and finger and pointed to the streak. "That's gold. And from the looks of it that line runs all the way through it."

Lucky you.

Holly's words to him when he'd sat on the rock appeared in his head. She'd known it was gold. And she'd given it to him anyway?

It didn't matter. Right now all the rock stood for was proof. Devon hadn't known to take the rock from his pocket because he hadn't known where it had come from. Wasn't aware that it had come from Holly's cave because the sheriff had never been there.

But Gramps' excitement over the rock sank in with a hefty dose of reality.

Maybe he wasn't crazy, maybe he had experienced the whole thing at the village with Holly and their time at the hot spring cave, but it changed nothing.

Holly was still involved in something he wanted no part of.

And now that he knew it wasn't a dream… he had to decide whether or not to go to the authorities.

***

Holly was at her desk four days later when she heard the announcement that her parents had returned to the compound. In an instant the air filled with the noise of multiple chairs being scooted back, voices, and palatable excitement because the head of their village was home.

Her parents had been gone for over two months and the community had missed them. It filled Holly's heart with joy to know she was part of a family so beloved, but at the same time she resented the constant observation. She imagined it was what Will and Kate felt, always beneath the world's scrutiny.

Except for the fact you don't have a Will. All you have is a heap of trouble about to smack you in the face.

Holly inhaled a calming breath before she left the office, grabbing her coat and the hat Ty had bought for her.

She traced the woven pattern with her thumb, unsure of why she wore it when it reminded her of what had happened and the things Ty had said to her in his condemning tone. "It's just a hat," she whispered. A hat like all the others in the mercantile.

And Ty's words were just words.

Hurtful barbs spawned from her lack of honesty with him. So because Ty had purchased the hat for her during a moment of caring and thankfulness toward her, she pulled it on over her hair as a reminder of who she was and the complicated nature of her life.

Ty was gone. It was for the best. But she wanted to hold onto what little of him he'd left behind.

The snowflakes stung a bit when they hit her skin, the winter wind brutally cold and crisp as always.

Laughter and excited chatter surrounded her as the villagers left their homes and the underground areas beneath the storage buildings to greet their leader. The center of the village quickly filled with people, one-thousand-eleven at last count. Smiling, cheering, happy people, heralding her parents' safe return.

The moment they saw Holly exiting her building to join in, the villagers parted to let her greet her parents.

Her father slowed the old-fashioned VW Snow-Trac to a stop and cut the engine. Painted white like all the vehicles in the village, the Snow-Trac had moving tracks like a bulldozer and the heated interior carried her parents comfortably through the winter cold, allowing them more freedom to travel to and from the secret landing strip located farther north.

With her mother's hand grasped firmly in his, Holly's father turned to face the crowd gathered around them. Holly pinned a smile to her face and hoped the makeup she wore hid the ravages of more than one sleepless night since Ty had left—was *taken*—from the cottage.

When she did sleep her dreams were filled with images of their time together. Wonderful, glorious dreams that slowly turned into an agonizing nightmare that left her chest tight and her eyes burning from tears she refused to shed.

She stepped forward to welcome her parents home, aware of the curious gazes watching her every move. "I've missed you, Mama. Papa."

She kissed her mother first and gave her a hug, then moved into her father's strong arms.

"We will talk soon, my girl. Stay close," he ordered.

Given her father's tone of voice, she wondered what Devon had said in his report. Or what had happened once Devon had carried Ty away. Devon would give her no answers when she asked, other than to say Ty still breathed and that was more than she needed to know.

After a full hour of greeting his village, Nikolas Klaas placed himself between his wife and daughter and began to slowly walk toward their home. It was a signal the villagers knew well and within a few steps the crowd fell away, recognizing that the homecoming was over.

Holly watched as the compound's inhabitants hurried back into the warmth of their cottages or into the buildings where they worked, and as quickly as they had appeared, the village center emptied, the town quickly becoming ghost-like in its sudden quiet.

"Come along, Holly," her father said, the words followed by a shallow cough.

"Are you all right?" Holly asked.

"Fine, fine. Just a little cold."

Her mother fussed over her father, asking one of the guards to retrieve a snowmobile to take Nikolas home.

Nikolas immediately grumbled but with a few soothing sounds and a stern yet loving look from Birgit, he quickly acquiesced.

Holly stopped in her tracks, the breath easing from her lungs in a slow, incredulous exhale. What she was seeing was love. True love. The kind that withstood the stress and pressures of life. Of *this* life.

And she wanted it.

She was strong. She had to be. But watching her parents interact, she realized she wanted someone she could lean on as well as fuss over.

And there was only one man who fit the description.

In that moment, standing in the cold on the trail leading toward the cottage, all she could think of was the fact that she had finally met the man who made her think of forever, who made her feel alive. Who made her laugh, think about the possibilities, the future.

But she couldn't have him?

Was she really supposed to give up *love*? Wasn't that the most important of God's commands?

"Holly? Are you coming?" her father asked.

"Yes, but— I just thought of something. Go home and rest from your trip."

"Holly, surely it can wait?" Her mother's expression gentled, the little lines on her face softening. "We need to talk about what happened while we were away."

"I know. We will, but—" Holly shook her head slowly back and forth, realizing the time may have come, but she wasn't ready. "Papa needs to rest and fight off that cold. I'll be home soon."

She could well imagine what Devon had told them but even though she wanted to set the story straight, her mind balked. She wasn't ready. She wasn't in the mood to be told her feelings for Ty had to end. Couldn't be real. Wouldn't last.

That the Elder Council would banish her to the north because she had brought Ty into their home. Banish her *forever* if she chose him.

She knew all those things.

But when she thought of the future...

Holly turned and hurried away, back toward the quiet building and the desk full of work. Another cave where she could hide and lick her wounds.

Better she gather her wits and spend her evening poring over the finalized printouts, than at home trying to say the words her father and the others would want to hear but not meaning any of them.

Somehow, she had to come up with a plan to forget she'd fallen in love.

***

Holly jerked upright when a hand gently landed on her shoulder.

"You didn't come home," her father said in his cold-gruff voice.

Holly blinked to clear the cobwebs from her mind and sat back, only then realizing she had fallen asleep at her desk. And having given Mari the firm order to not be disturbed before closing her office door, she hadn't been. "Sorry."

Nikolas looked around her somewhat cluttered office before walking over to stand in front of the fireplace. The logs had burned down but her father stoked them, adding a few pieces of wood to chase the chill from the room.

"Your mother sent your favorite soup. And Anna sent cookies. Eat," he ordered.

"I'm not very hungry."

"Anna says you have said that for several days now. But your Papa is home and I say you can eat—or you can talk. Which would you rather do?"

Considering he always had a twinkle in his eye whenever she was around and had doted on Holly her entire life, she knew the order was born out of love. "Fine," she said as she opened the thermos of soup and inhaled the wonderful fragrance.

Her father left the fire and made himself at home on the sofa lining the wall across from her desk.

"Start at the beginning."

"I thought I was supposed to eat?" Her father's eyes narrowed on her and she squirmed a bit beneath his stare. "There was a plane crash."

"Before that."

Stifling a groan, she slurped some of the soup to buy some time. "I was at the cave—and, no, I wasn't supposed to travel in such bad weather but Ty's— The pilot's distress call came over the radio and I couldn't ignore it. Papa, I had to do something. I had to see if he'd survived the crash." She lifted her chin and met her father's gaze. "He wouldn't have. Ty was unconscious when I got there and he would have frozen to death before Devon and his men could get to the scene."

Her father folded his hands over his belly and settled deeper into the comfortable cushions of the couch. "You have feelings for this man. More than your feelings for Devon?"

Unable to lie, she nodded. "Yes, very much so. Devon is… just a friend." One presently on her bad side.

She sipped more of the soup to give her nervous hands and rambling mouth something to do.

After returning to her office this afternoon she had paced for hours, trying to resign herself to the future and the decision of the Elder Council. But something inside her rebelled and demanded more, adding to her battle of wills. "And I know what you're going to say."

"Do you, now?"

"Yes. You're going to say the best relationships build on friendships first, but what about when that friend is more like a brother? An older, cranky brother."

Her father chuckled before he stopped himself and regarded her with a raised eyebrow.

"Papa, you like Devon and so do I. Sometimes. But more than that, you want me to make amends with Devon and apologize for the things I said about his methods for removing Ty from the village. But I won't. I *can't*," she stressed. "What Devon did was wrong. I can't believe *you* would condone such a thing."

"Normally I wouldn't. Force is rarely *ever* used but in this case I believe Devon did what was best."

Holly rolled her eyes. Of course her father would agree with Devon. The Elder

Council was made up primarily of men. Men who stuck together like glue when it came to issues such as this.

Her father cleared his throat and the act turned into a series of coughs. Holly got to her feet and went to pour him some water. "You should be resting, Papa. Besides, there is no need to worry about me or Ty McGarretty. He's gone," she said, dropping to her knees at her father's feet. "So now it's over. Done."

"I'm afraid it's not. The Elder Council has confirmed the meeting tomorrow evening, to decide your punishment for bringing the pilot into the village."

"I see." She had hoped given the weather and time constraints they faced the meeting would be postponed, at least for a while. Long enough for her to gather her emotions where Ty was concerned.

"Try not to worry. Love is a very powerful emotion, Holly. The greatest."

She blinked at him, more than a bit confused since she certainly hadn't told her father that she was in love with Ty. "I'm not following."

"The elders love you, my dear. Just remind them of our purpose and goals, show them your grace and mercy for doing a good deed for another human, and you'll have them eating out of your hands."

"Enough that they'll forgive all?" she quipped, doubtful of the possibility.

"You never know. But it is the season of forgiveness."

CHAPTER TWELVE

Later that same evening Holly stroked the brush down Moxie's back and the bristles made a rasping sound that nearly, but not quite, drowned out Moxie's snoring.

Moxie loved being brushed and groomed, and whenever Holly felt out of sorts, the kennel was the only place in the compound where she wasn't being watched or judged, only loved. "Are you going to stand there and stare at me all night?" she asked, never taking her gaze off her pet.

"Depends. Are you going to let me apologize?" Devon asked, moving toward her.

"Depends," she repeated, feeling more than a bit snarky. "Are you actually sorry?"

Moxie lifted her head from atop Holly's knee and regarded Devon with a drowsy yet intense stare. No doubt because Devon had disturbed the dog's peaceful stint of relaxation.

"I'm sorry...that I let my temper get the best of me," he said. "When I heard you had taken him to your cave, I got angry."

"You think?" Holly paused in her brushing and earned a quick head tilt from Moxie. She set the brush aside and ran her fingers through Moxie's fur, gaining comfort from the feel.

Devon squatted down close to them and stared into Holly's eyes. Sorry or not, she wanted to yell at him, shove him, hurt him because she was hurting so badly.

"Do it," he said. "I know you want to."

"You have no idea what I want," she said wearily.

"You want him. And considering you've barely said a word to any of us since I took McGarretty out of here, I'd say you're angry enough to give me what-for."

Oh, she was definitely that. Angry and sad and so disappointed. Heart-broken. "I should have kept to my sixth grade mantra of how boys are stupid. Maybe then..."

"You wouldn't be in here hiding?"

Hiding? Holly shoved him backward. Devon teetered for a second before he landed on his butt.

She knew him, knew his reflexes and she *knew* he had deliberately left himself open and vulnerable. Didn't matter. Seeing him sprawled out on the kennel floor *did* give her a not-so-nice thrill. "I'm caring for my dogs. What are you doing here besides giving me a hard time?"

"I came to say goodbye."

She blinked at the news. "What? Where are you going?"

"New York first. Who knows where later. I just finished meeting with your father. I asked him for reassignment and he's granted it."

"I'm... I don't know what to say. I'm shocked." This was Devon's home every bit as much as it was hers. He was just going to leave? *Not leave. Reassignment. There's a big difference.*

Devon righted himself, one knee braced on the floor. "It's the right decision, especially since your response to the news wasn't to ask me to stay."

"You deserve better than me, Dev," she said, meaning every word. "You are a good man. A hard-working, handsome, wonderful, pain-in-the-butt...but a good man. We may not always agree but you deserve someone who loves you for you."

"So do you, Ms. Klaas."

Devon rose to his full height. He held out his hand to help her up but once she stood in front of him, Holly stepped forward and wrapped her arms around his waist, lifted her head and kissed his cheek. "Goodbye, Dev. Be safe."

Devon rested his chin on top of her head. "Goodbye, Holly. Be happy."

Holly stood there and watched as Devon left the kennel as quietly as he'd entered it.

Happy? How would she ever be happy when things were so screwed up?

"The elders love you. Just remind them of our purpose and goals, show them your grace and mercy for doing what you felt was right, and you'll have them eating out of your hands," her Papa had said.

She leaned against the wood enclosure behind her and bowed her head. *God, please, show me the way. Tell me what to do. Show me. Help me. I can't do this without You.*

An idea blasted into her head. It was crazy but— Crazy enough to work?

It could. It *had* to. Because crazy was not following her heart and giving up on something so precious. Because crazy was letting others strip her of love when her birth had already decided a big portion of her future all ready.

Was she just going to accept whatever the Elder Council decided? Really? Or was she going to trust in God and have faith that she'd figure out a way?

Holly rushed from the kennel, wanting to get the dogs ready but needing to do other things first. She'd need supplies, a way to get to Anchorage.

Would she even be able to convince Ty to see her? Talk to her?

Was she really going to risk *everything*?

Let us hold fast the profession of our faith without wavering.

The verse came to her as clearly as the plan had mere seconds ago. She had faith. Faith in God, faith in her Savior. Faith in the knowledge she'd done what was right by saving Ty. And as the future leader, she needed to do what was right for her people. Without wavering.

Holly hurried into the house and down the hall to the room opposite hers, passing her parents' bedroom on the way. She could hear low murmurs on the other side of their door, probably her father filling her mother in on the details of Devon's plans.

Holly entered Anna's room and tiptoed to the bed. "Anna? Anna, wake up," she urged, careful to keep quiet and praying her aunt wouldn't startle and scream. "Anna?"

"What? What is it?" Anna asked quietly, her voice sleep-rough.

"I need your help." Holly sat on the bed. She trembled with the force of her feelings, her determination. Struggled to keep her fear at bay.

Was she really going to do this? What if it was all for nothing? If Anna sounded the alarm?

"What's wrong, child? What time is it?"

Holly found Anna's hand and grasped it, squeezing. "It doesn't matter. Anna, do you miss Ben?"

"Oh, child… What are you doing?"

"Do you miss Ben? Do you want to see your son?"

"Of course I do. What mother doesn't want to see her child?"

Holly squeezed Anna's fingers. "Then you have to help me."

"I'm not liking the sound of this, Holly Elizabeth. What are you up to?"

Holly struggled to find the words, wondering how much to say. "I have to talk to Ty. I have to see him one last time."

"No."

"*Yes*. Anna… I love him. I *love* him, enough that if the Elder Council can't accept it—"

"Don't say it. Oh, Holly, *no*."

"It's all right. I'm not leaving, not for good. I'll be back because I refuse to let them take my future away from me. But without Ty…" She let her voice trail off, reminding herself that all *would* be well.

"It's not possible, child."

"With God anything is possible. Isn't that what you're always telling me? Anna, come on. Are you seriously okay with accepting a lifetime of absence just because they're not *allowed* to come back? Surely there's another way?"

For the first time since Holly entered Anna's bedroom her aunt was quiet.

"What do you want me to do?"

Holly closed her eyes and said a quick prayer of thanks, shivering from the surge of joy and courage jolting through her.

"Cover for me. Tell everyone I left to spend some time with the dogs. I'll be back for the council meeting."

"Oh, child, it's the dark of night."

Holly muffled a laugh. "It's dark no matter what time of day it is, Anna."

"Don't sass me, child."

"Never," she said, kissing Anna's cheek. "I'll be extra careful. And I'll be back tomorrow," she promised, wondering what the next twenty-four hours had in store for her considering she didn't really have a plan, only a purpose. *Faith.* "Oh, and, Anna? Take a batch of your special punch to the guardhouse tomorrow at *exactly* 4 o'clock." She pressed the glass vial of powder Devon had left behind in her office into Anna's hand. "Add this."

"Oh, Holly. Are you sure? What if Devon is on duty? He's not leaving for several days yet."

All the better. She loved Devon but— "Good. I think Devon and the guards need a taste of their own medicine, don't you?"

***

Why had he agreed to this?

Ty lowered himself onto the chair in front of the group of little kids gathered for the library's story time and glared at Gramps when he leaned over and whispered something into the librarian's ear. Apparently the woman was one of the many who'd brought food to the house and helped Gramps keep the kids entertained while Ty was gone. And this? This was Gramps' way of saying thanks—by volunteering Ty to play Santa because the hired Santa had shown up drunk and smelling of fish.

Ty had stopped into the library after visiting his insurance company so he could get a few pictures of Logan and Abbie on Santa's lap. Instead of photos, ten minutes later he found himself inside the suit and sweating beneath all the padding and fake hair.

He did his best to ignore the rambunctious kids anxious to sit on his lap and opened the book shoved into his hands. *The Night Before Christmas*. At least it was one he knew. His grandmother had read the story to them every year on Christmas Eve, even when he and Beth were teens.

Trying to see through the finger-smudged fake spectacles perched on his nose and batting the white beard out of his mouth, he began reading. The kids settled down several pages in and once he got into the flow of things, Ty was able to ignore Gramps' smirk. The old man was getting his own form of payback for all the worry Ty had put him through.

A latecomer arrived and the blast of cold Alaskan air cooled Ty's overheated cheeks. He kept reading but when the little hairs on the back of his neck tingled, he glanced up, seeing nothing unusual in the line of adults waiting in the back of the room.

Ty finished the story and then sat through the process of a dozen kids climbing onto his lap to give him their Christmas wishes while the parents took massive amounts of digital photos. He breathed a sigh of relief when the librarian said Santa had to leave.

"T—uh, Santa? I'm going to take the munchkins across the street to get something to eat," Gramps said.

Ty lifted his gloved hand in response and hurried to get out of the itchy beard and suit. Fifteen minutes later he'd turned in the suit and been abundantly thanked and propositioned by the librarian's assistant when he saw a woman by the door, waiting?

She was slim and blond and— "Holly?"

The woman turned and smiled at him, her expression soft and moderately sardonic. Pleased?

"You were a wonderful Santa, Ty."

***

Finding the patience to wait on Ty to finish his Santa duties was one of the hardest things Holly had ever had to do. She'd stood there and listened to his deep voice, watched the way the children responded to him as he read the popular story, all the while imagining more. So much more.

This wasn't an untrustworthy man.

While he read the book she had never, ever liked, she'd focused on the timbre of his voice and knew without a doubt that she was following God's plan for her.

The time spent piecing together puzzles, watching movies and playing checkers, talking—so much talking—had created emotions within her that were so strong she was afraid to give them voice. Afraid to believe. But that was exactly what she was being called to do. She had to believe with the faith of the children who had just left the library.

"What are you doing here?"

"Surprised?" she asked, trying to calm the rapid beat of her heart.

"You could say that."

"Ty, I'm sorry. About how things... ended."

Ty made a derisive sound, as though the shock of her appearance was wearing off and the realization of their last conversation about the compound's secrets sank in.

She had so much to tell him. Show him. Get him to believe.

"What are you doing here?"

His voice held a hard edge but she saw the way his gaze softened when he looked at her. Like he'd missed her?

The feeling was certainly mutual.

She'd dressed carefully for this meeting. Rather than the snowsuit she had left behind in the Inuit village with her sled team, she'd ignored the cold and chosen a black thigh-length sweater dress and shiny, spiky black boots that ended just above her knees, leaving about an inch of leg visible. A deep red swing coat gave her a bit of a dramatic flare, but it kept her warm and cozy.

Maybe dressing in such a way wasn't playing fair, but she needed all the feminine armor at her disposal to protect herself from the pain Ty was capable of inflicting if he—

Believe.

She stiffened her spine and hoped Ty could forgive her. Prayed that he cared for her enough to listen and hear her out. And, God willing, work by her side for all they needed to accomplish year after year. "I am sorry, Ty. Especially about how Devon..."

"Sucker punched me? Or do you mean how he *drugged* me?"

"Both. I had no idea he was going to do that. I didn't know he even had such a thing in his possession."

Ty stared at her a long moment before some of the tension holding his shoulders tight seemed to ease.

"What do you want, Holly?"

Spying the librarian behind Ty, she tilted her head toward the door. "Walk with me?"

"I'm meeting Gramps and the kids. What do you want?"

Time to woman-up and say what she'd come to say. "You were right when you said I expected you to trust me, but I wasn't willing to trust you in return."

"You're going to have to do better than that, sweetheart. Tell me something I don't already know."

"Okay. The something you don't know is that—I want a second chance. I'm serious," she said when she saw him grimace. Grimacing in response to her statement?

That wasn't good.

"What's changed?"

"Everything," she said, lowering her voice so the words didn't carry. "Ty, you didn't contact the authorities. That means—"

"It means I don't want you to spend your life in prison."

Which meant that he cared for her, too. But Ty had to do more than care. He had to love her so much, love their cause and their God so much, Ty was willing to sacrifice his current life and dedicate himself to serve.

She needed to share enough information with him to convince him to trust her, come back with her to the compound, but not enough to leave him scoffing at her.

How much to say? How much to withhold? No matter how many times she'd rehearsed this moment in her head, she hadn't come up with a clear path to approach the crux of the matter. "Before you say no, hear me out. Please," she added when it looked as though he wanted to balk. "Ty, I need your help to convince the Elder Council that...you're trustworthy."

His gaze narrowed, his lashes lowering over his beautiful eyes as he contemplated her words.

"Are you saying you're going to confront them?"

Oh, please give me strength. "Yes. Ty, I care for you a-and I think you care for me, too."

"No kidding. As much as I hate to admit it, you're right about that."

Before she could be pleased by his admission, he walked by her and shoved his way out the door.

She followed him to the sidewalk.

"Do you know I thought I'd dreamt it all? That I thought I was going crazy until I found that memory rock you gave me? Then I wished I *had* dreamt it."

The words pierced her heart. "I never meant to hurt you, or for you to *get* hurt. "Ty, I'll tell you everything. *Show* you everything."

Ty stepped off the curb into the street but stopped in front of a parked car, his back to her. He didn't turn.

"Why would you do that?"

This is it. He's waiting. Say it, or regret it for the rest of your life. Believe! "Because I love you. I know it sounds crazy and rushed, but it's true. And even if you don't believe me, believe this— I am risking everything to be here right now. Just so I can tell you how much you mean to me."

Ty turned to face her. "Are you talking banishment again?"

She nodded, aware of the stares of people passing them on the sidewalk. Aware and not caring.

This mattered. Ty mattered. "If you come with me, you'll understand why I did what I did. But I have to *show* you. Seeing is believing."

His expression revealed his conflicting emotions. "I'm just supposed to take off with you again? After what happened last time?"

Holly hurried after Ty, across the street, earning the honk of a horn for her jaywalking. "Please."

He stopped with his hand on the door of the diner.

Holly followed Ty's gaze to where George and the children sat at a table inside. Logan and Abbie were beautiful children. Gramps a character. It would be so easy to love them. "Ty, *you* said trust runs both ways. I made a mistake when I didn't trust you enough to tell you the truth, but I'm here *now*. I'm asking you to forgive me. I'm *trusting* you. I'm trusting *in* you. You said you would help me and I'm here because… I'm holding you to your word."

Ty loosened his grip on the door and faced her. "Holly, it's almost Christmas and those kids have already been through more than any kid should have to face. I can't leave now. I can't leave them. I couldn't get back in time for Christmas. Think about what you're asking."

He was right. No one should miss Christmas morning. Especially the little family that had been so battered and torn by life. "Bring them," she said, feeling as surprised as Ty looked by the statement. She nodded, though, refusing to let anything stop her.

If she was going to change the way things were done, she had to do whatever it took. *If you're going to be a bear, be a grizzly.* How many times had her father said that to her? "I mean it. Bring them, too. I give you my word you will *all* be safe."

"You can't promise that," he muttered. "And to take the kids…"

"Okay, fine. Maybe I can't promise there won't be a lot of yelling and upset and maybe a punch or two thrown but… the kids will be safe. The last thing anyone there would want to do is ruin their Christmas."

Ty ran a hand over his face, silent for several long seconds.

"I've got to be insane to consider this."

Ty gave her a hard stare and Holly held her breath, waiting for his answer. *Please, please, please.*

"Nothing illegal? No guns, no drugs, no human trafficking, *nothing*?"

She held his gaze, wondering if the earth was really shifting on its axis or if it just felt like it to her. "*No*. Absolutely not."

"But you can't just tell me what's there?"

She smiled at the complaint she heard in his tone. "You wouldn't believe me, not after everything that's happened," she argued. "Ty, you wanted to see the buildings for yourself, and I'll show you. But more than anything, we have to convince the Elder Council to change. Please help me."

The sounds and sights and scents of Christmas surrounded them. Nuts roasting in cinnamon and sugar from a street vendor on the corner outside the bank. The colorful lights in the bushes lining the walk. Bells jingling. It was Christmas. The celebration of Christ's birth and all the love and hope and joy He brought to earth and his people.

She wanted to bring those same qualities home to *her* people, reward the village that gave so much for so little in return.

Ty lowered his chin to his chest and grimaced. "Ahhh. No one could ever say bush pilots are sane."

Joy flooded her but she couldn't celebrate—not yet. "You'll do it? You'll travel to the village with me?"

"Yeah." He groaned. "How hard can it be to drag two kids and an old man through the Alaskan bush."

CHAPTER THIRTEEN

Ty wasn't sure what to expect when they finally made it back to Holly's cottage.

Getting there took some doing. Since his purchase of a new plane wasn't completed, they borrowed a buddy's plane and took it north, leaving it in a village consisting of exactly four homes and a hangar. From there, they took three snowmobiles to another, smaller outpost where they boarded a Snowtrac for Gramps' sake and the kids', using it to travel over some of Alaska's harshest terrain.

Like it or not, his admiration for the beautiful woman at his side grew even though it was tempered by his unease at whatever she was going to show him inside those buildings. But to have gone through what she had to make the admittedly difficult trip to get him... To say she *loved* him?

Find out what's in those buildings before making any declarations.

The flight and time spent traveling over the snow had given him plenty of space to think about the potential outcomes. Problem was he wasn't sure which one he favored most.

He could see himself creating a future with Holly, but he wasn't a man who could sacrifice his morals. Not even for love.

Whatever she was about to show him had to be on the up-and-up and if it wasn't... He had to stick to his guns and say goodbye.

No matter what.

They approached the village around three-thirty that afternoon. Unlike before when Holly made obvious efforts to keep him from learning the way, this time she didn't try any tricks. But he knew only time would tell if he could do whatever it was she wanted of him.

"We have to go the rest of the way on foot. Stay close and be quiet. We have to get in without anyone seeing us or I won't be able to get you inside the buildings."

Yeah, the rules thing. Whatever. Not for the first time, he questioned the wisdom of bringing an old man and two kids along for the ride.

"We'll go to the cottage first. Anna will take care of your grandfather and the children while we go into the village. Okay?"

He didn't like the idea of being separated but the last thing they needed was for Abbie to wake up grumpy from her nap. "That's fine. Let's go."

Ty carried Abbie and followed Holly's lead, letting Gramps and Logan bring up the rear. Before long Ty was able to see the shadows cast by the villagers' homes thanks to the moon overhead. The darkness hid their presence, the crunch of snow beneath their boots masked by the wind blowing in the pines.

Holly took the group to the cottage from the back, entering the kitchen where Anna cooked.

"Holly, you're ba— Oh!"

Anna's eyes widened when she took in Holly's guests.

"Oh, Holly."

Holly rushed forward, her finger pressed to her lips in case her parents were home. "He wouldn't come without them, Anna."

"Holly, you didn't tell me you had such a beautiful sister."

Ty looked at Gramps in surprise, struggling to contain his embarrassment. With everything going on and them sneaking around like they were, Gramps chose now to flirt?

"Where's Mama and Papa?" Holly asked.

"Your mother is visiting Darcy at the infirmary, and your father is in the second, uh, building," Anna said.

"Perfect. And you did what I asked?"

"Yes, but I doubt it will last long."

"Okay," Holly said. "We need to hurry. Will you watch the children with George while Ty and I go into the village?"

"Yes. Yes, of course. Oh, Holly, are you sure this is going to work?"

"It has to," Holly said. "For all of our sakes. Ty? Let's go."

Back outside, Holly stuck to the trees off the paths and skirted the backside of the storage buildings.

When they saw the coast was clear, she punched in a code, unlocking the door.

Inside, all was quiet but Holly held a finger to her lips and motioned for him to follow. Quickly.

She peeked around a corner and stopped. When she hesitated, Ty pulled her back to check out the scene himself, smirking when he saw the camo-dressed guards snoozing. Some were at desks, others on couches in a lounge area. But each and every one of them was asleep. "How did you manage that?" he whispered against her ear.

"Anna's punch," she said simply. "Come on."

Holly led him to a set of double doors positioned beneath the stairwell and punched in another code but the moment she took a step toward them he stopped her. "Wait."

She tilted her head to one side and regarded him with a slight crook to her mouth.

"You're right to be nervous," she said bluntly. "There's no going back."

"Yeah, that statement helps."

She gave him a wry grin. "Ty? There's no going back for me, either. Just remember that before you jump to conclusions."

The moment the door opened Ty was amazed by the size of the room expanding beyond a windowed wall. It had to be a hundred thousand square feet. More? All underground and invisible from the sky.

Impossible.

Holly made sure the door didn't bang shut. "This way," she whispered. "Hurry. There's a room up here where we can stop but we can't let them see us. All of them may not be sleeping."

When he didn't move, Holly took his hand in hers and tugged him along behind her while he dragged his feet and took in their surroundings. "This isn't possible."

The area below them was a veritable madhouse of boxes and people. More people than he'd ever seen around the village the entire time he had been there. Where had they been? What were they— His gaze narrowed, focused, but none of it made sense.

"Come on," Holly urged, tugging harder on his hand. "You have a lot to see."

"The building... How...?"

"Most of the building is underground," she said, confirming his earlier thoughts. "It merges with the other two storage buildings beneath the mountain."

Storage. Yeah, there was a lot to store. "Holly, wait. What am I looking at?"

Her impatience showed when she stopped, glancing around them as though Devon or one of his men was going to jump out at them any second.

"We are in the middle of...delivery preparation."

"Delivery of what?"

"Items. For Christmas morning," she added, looking at him intently, like she waited for him to catch onto whatever it was she was saying but— No, his brain wasn't going there. That would mean he *was* insane. Because it was insane to think that. Royally, certifiably, shut-him-in-a-padded-room insane.

"Ty... Do you believe in Christmas?"

"You've got to be kidding me," he said, his voice rising with his anger. Holly quickly shushed him but it didn't stop the fury flowing through his veins. He'd come all this way, dragging Gramps and the kids along, for her to stand there and pretend this place was *Santa Land*? "That's what you're going with? You're going to stand there and try to get me to swallow that load of lies?"

"Look down there. What do you see?"

"A warehouse full of stolen merchandise."

"*No*. What you see is Christmas. You see the presents from Secret Santas, the ones someone *thinks* someone else took the time and effort and expense to buy and the other person is too embarrassed to admit they didn't. The cars charities receive from unnamed benefactors to help those in need? Us. The toys so generously found at orphanages Christmas morning? *Us*. The blankets and coats for the homeless, the food for the shelters, immunizations for countries that have been *forgotten* by the rest of the world. Presents that appear out of nowhere for those who are broken and lonely and sad? All of it comes from us."

He stared down at the well-ordered chaos taking place. Boxes being packed, people working. Normal people. Not elves. "So you accept donations and redistribute them? You're a charity." That had to be it, right?

Holly made a sound of frustration and shook her head, her arms crossing over her chest. "No. We're not."

"So this isn't the North Pole?"

She flinched at his sarcasm. "Of course not. It's Alaska. But you are standing in one of Santa's Workshops," she added with a wavering smile.

"Those people aren't elves, Holly."

"No. Elves are a myth. Just part of a story from long ago to make it more fun."

"More fun?" he repeated, too dazed to do more than that.

"Ty, how was I supposed to show you this, and you not think the worst? Either that we're all crazy—or thieves? I couldn't share this with you, not having just met you."

"But you're telling me now."

She nodded, her expressions changing as rapidly as the thoughts barreling through his head.

"Yes, I am. Ty, can you imagine what would happen if the world found out about us? Look at what Christmas has become. It's a mad rush of overspending, greed, anxiety and cynicism. Some celebrate it as a holiday without giving a single thought to the *reason* it exists, to the true meaning of love. To think that there really are places like this where we *give* the stuff away... It would bring all of those people crashing down on our heads because most *everyone* would want a piece of the pie."

"Wait— You said *places*. Are you saying there's more than one?" He didn't know what to call it. "Another...workshop?"

Holly took his hand and pulled him down the hallway, deeper into the building.

"There are three located in climates similar to this one. The reason for the rules about no outsiders? It was because the North Pole location was discovered when my seventh great-grandfather *Nikolas II* was in charge."

"Yeah, and reindeer fly."

"No, that's a myth, too," she said. "Follow me. This way."

"Tell me about Nik The Second," he ordered, giving her a disgruntled look.

"The location was discovered by some lost adventurists. The men were sworn to secrecy, but one was known to drink. Later, an acquaintance of that man wrote a tale about a man in a red suit—which happened to be my great-grandfather's pajamas. They were fur-trimmed for warmth."

Okay. Yeah, he could buy that.

Seriously?

"Ty, I'm telling you the truth."

Ty stared around him in a daze, trying to take it all in while they moved deeper into the building hidden beneath the mountain. "Where are the other locations?"

"One is in a desert, two on small islands in the South Pacific, one in the Amazon—they really have to stop cutting down the rainforest—and one in New York City."

Ty laughed at that—until he realized she wasn't joking. For real? He was supposed to believe that? "I lived in New York six years. I don't ever remember seeing Santa's Workshop."

Holly stared up at him. "Ty, do you *really* think the New York underground is filled with snakes, rats and freed alligators?"

He'd heard those rumors. Had been warned not to ever go below ground. But every adult told their kid that to keep them from danger.

"Mayor G discovered us during his second year in office but my father convinced him to keep our secret. He's a regular visitor to that location now, but he doesn't know *any*thing about the others. You are the only person who knows outside of our organization."

"Mayor G?" Surely she didn't mean…

She nodded. "He likes to visit and de-stress. I've never met him but Papa says he's quite nice. Maybe if we are ever there at the same time we can arrange an introduction.

Oh, but... Devon is moving there now so you might not want to go, I suppose."

Introduce him to Mayor G? Devon was *moving* there? "I thought no one left the compound?"

"We may request transfers to other locations and if approved, it's allowed. But one of the rules is if you choose the *outside* world, you have to stay there."

Ty listened to Holly's words but couldn't seem to focus on them, not when he was bombarded by the rapid-fire chaos of his thoughts.

And then it hit him— Had she said *Papa*?

There was a shelving unit positioned outside a door. Ty glanced down as they passed and he noted the boxes were labeled, first by country, then city, then address, most of which were charities, orphanages and the like. "You're saying your father...is *Santa Claus*?"

"Yes," she said, looking at him over her shoulder. "At least until he retires."

"*Santa* is retiring?"

"No, not technically. My father is retiring, but because it's a family business handed down from generation to generation, eventually I'll be the new girl in red."

Thanks to seeing the labels he was *this close* to believing Holly's story about delivering goods for those in need but that last statement ruined it all. "Santa is male, sweetheart."

"You're being sexist now? Really?"

His smile grew as Holly stood there and glared at him with feminist attitude at his statement. In the end she smacked a hand against his chest, her face flushed a hot, hot pink, and stalked off in a huff.

"What, come on," Ty said, barely able to choke the words out. "You expect me to keep a straight face after you say *that*? Holly?" A few chuckles emerged and he tried to disguise them as coughs. "Stop. I have an important question. Come on, stop."

Holly paused and glanced over her shoulder, her expression a mix of irritation and frustration. "What?"

"Does this mean Devon is the Head *Elf*?"

***

Holly walked away from Ty, at a loss as to how to get that look off his face, and yet struggling to contain her own amusement at his Devon comment. "Devon isn't the head elf. He was head of security here, though now I suppose one of his guards will be getting a promotion."

"Ah, man, I don't get to spring my joke on him? Please?"

"Do you want to get punched again?" she asked, knowing exactly how well that nickname would go over.

"I'd like to see him try it. I guarantee this time won't be so easy."

Just what she needed, for Ty and Devon to be brawling while she was trying to explain to the Elder Council why Ty should—what? Be allowed to stay?

Panic filled her. What if Ty didn't *want* to stay? Didn't believe her?

"So how exactly does Santa deliver all the presents in one night?" Ty asked, his tone mocking.

Forcing herself to focus, she shoved her hair over her shoulder and inhaled. "Multiple Santas, just like everyone says. The real ones are Klaas relatives, though. Everyone has a region and a leader for their group, but they all report to my father who is the direct descendent."

"I see," he drawled, chuckling, reaching out to brush her hair off her face and reveal her left ear.

"What are you doing?"

"Looking for pointy ears. Wait, Holl— You have really cute ears. Doesn't that count for something? They're small, like seashells. Where are you going?"

She didn't pause. Ty made fun of her. *Still* believed they were some sort of good Samaritan charity rather than the real deal. And why would he think differently? Television had depicted Santa's workshop as a bright, colorful factory with happily singing elves.

The people here were happy. Mostly. There was the whole outsider/rule issue but as a whole everyone considered themselves not only blessed but fortunate to be born into the organization. It felt good to help others, especially on such a large scale.

Still, she had one last bit of proof left to show Ty, one that would leave him without any doubts.

She didn't bother turning around to make sure Ty followed her. She knew he was there because every now and then yet another irritating chuckle emerged from his chest.

Stupid man. Was it so difficult to believe that goodness and generosity still existed

in the world? That some people believed
in the greater good and the magic of
Christmas found in the love and sacrifice
and generosity first displayed by God?

She punched in the security code and
waited for the hiss of air that indicated the
hydraulic door locks released.

"That sounded impressive. How do you
power that?"

She rolled her eyes that Ty would be a
typical man to ooh and ahh over simple
mechanics and stepped aside with a wave
of her hand over the sensor. One by one the
lights snapped on throughout the building
but she didn't watch them transform the
dark room into a bright, well-equipped
hangar. Instead she watched Ty's face,
waiting for the moment it dawned on him
that maybe, just maybe, she wasn't making
this up.

It took all of two seconds. One for his
eyes to adjust to the brighter lights and two
to zero in on the sleigh—a fanciful and
elaborately designed, deep, glorious red with
silver gilded rims and etched sides.

"That's... That's a massive…."

"Yes it is," she quipped, heading toward
the craft.

Ty's longer stride allowed him to beat her there, and he stared at the instrument panel like a kid in a candy store.

That's when Holly knew she had him. With time the reality of what she had tried to tell him, *show him*, would sink in but it had taken the sight of Santa's sleigh to convince Ty that the impossible was indeed possible.

What was it about boys and their toys? She would find it amusing if they weren't running out of time. The Elder Council meeting was scheduled to start in...*ten minutes*?

Her stomach flip-flopped, making her ill. Ty had to believe her. Believe *in* her.

Did he think she hadn't noticed the fact he hadn't said he loved her? She didn't want to rush him or for him to say something he didn't mean but a little reassurance would go a long way to easing her anxiety.

Faith, she reminded herself.

"That's... Wow." Ty turned his head to look at her, his expression a mix of confoundedness and awe. "It *flies*?"

"Like a personalized flying carpet."

"How? I don't even recognize some of this technology."

"Santa has his secrets," she said automatically but when Ty continued to stare at her in expectation she crossed her arms over her chest. "Ty, governments do not spend five hundred thousand dollars on screwdrivers and wrenches. This sleigh and all of the others were gifts because of my family's dedication to our cause and keeping hope alive in a dark world."

"You've flown it?"

"Not by myself, but yes. Learning to fly this has been part of my training."

Ty was caught up in the moment and the awe of all she'd shown him. But when the novelty wore off and reality set in, what then? "Ty, I've thrown you a curve ball. I get it. But there's more to this life than the sleigh and the fun of Christmas.

"Growing up, I resented the fact that all the other kids got to be with their families on Christmas Eve and Christmas morning. When Papa returned he was so tired and worn out from the deliveries that he'd sleep most of the day," she said, trailing her fingers over the silvery edge of the sleigh. "I didn't like it that I had to wait to open my presents, that our Christmas celebration was delayed because of everyone else. Selfish, huh?"

"You were a kid. It's understandable," Ty said, climbing into the sleigh and sitting in the pilot's seat.

He looked good there. Like he belonged. And her heart squeezed a bit at the sight.

Ty scanned the controls and devices, his big, capable hands learning the shape and placement of all the buttons and levers that drove her so batty. She was much more interested in delivering the presents than flying the sleigh. The Elder Council meeting is about to begin. We have to go."

Ty's hands stilled on the central control system, and his expression lost some of the joy of discovery.

"What are they going to say now that you've shown me this? Would they really banish you?"

"Yes. But if I can convince them that the future of our village depends on their children and grandchildren's happiness... Of being free to choose the life we want without losing what matters most..." She glanced at her watch. "Ty, I understand if you say no to all of this. My future was set the moment I was conceived and it's easy for me to defend my family tradition. But for you, if we can convince the Elder Council at all, it means secrets and sacrifices."

Ty turned on the seat and leaned across to open the passenger side door for her. "Get in."

She hesitated a moment—they *really* had to go—but then she slid onto the luxurious velvet bench beside him, closing the door with a soft *click* of the latch.

Ty leaned his elbow on the seat back behind them, staring into her eyes with an expression she couldn't read.

"This is your big secret? You're not holding anything else back?"

She blinked at him. "You don't think this is enough?"

"It most definitely is. But how do we convince the...?"

"Elder Council," she said.

"Yeah," Ty said. "How do we get them to trust me? This is about those adventurists betraying the secret, right?"

"It certainly is," Devon said from the doorway, flanked by two of his guards. "Let's see what the Elders have to say about this betrayal. Both of you come with us."

CHAPTER FOURTEEN

Holly glared at Devon as she and Ty exited the sleigh and approached the blocked doorway.

"Keep your hands to yourselves," she warned softly, making eye contact with each of them but lingering on Devon. "Understood?"

Oh, he looked angry. Furious. But she'd expected no less.

She and Ty walked ahead of the others, leaving the structure and crossing the street to the church and schoolhouse building where all the Elder Council meetings were held.

Getting caught by Devon wasn't part of the plan but apparently that wasn't the only surprise awaiting them when they walked into the room.

Her mother and Anna were there, as well as George and the children. Abbie still looked sleepy and was snuggled on Birgit's lap, while Logan sat between his great-grandfather and Anna. Holly locked gazes with her mother and mouthed, *I'm sorry, Mama.*

Her mother's arms tightened around the precious little girl. Birgit lowered her cheek to Abbie's head, the hug and snuggle an obvious gesture meant to relay a message.

"What have you to say for yourself, daughter?" Nikolas said.

Her father's bushy white eyebrows were lowered over his eyes and she braced herself for his censure. That was the thing with her Papa. Never a man to raise his voice except in laughter, sometimes the quietness of his anger proved more wounding. He had been able to forgive her for saving Ty, but to do what she'd done tonight...

Please give me the words, God. I need You.

She took a deep breath and faced those gathered. "I say... it's time to reevaluate how we live."

She heard disgruntled murmurs and surprised gasps from the crowd, but lifted her chin and continued. "I am aware the punishment for bringing an outsider into our village is to be banished North. The goal of sending the person to that location is to make them aware of the danger we face as a community because of what happened in the past."

"And yet you not only brought a man here weeks ago, you then returned and brought him and his family back?" one of the Elders demanded.

"Yes. I did. And I'd do it again, too," she said, struggling to keep her voice from shaking.

"Holly," her father warned, his gaze begging her to take care.

"My reason is born of love. I did the right thing by rescuing Ty. I showed kindness and mercy to someone in trouble," she said, making a point of looking at Ty before addressing the Elder Council again. "Isn't that what we're called to do? Not once in our lives but always. And in our case, year round? Isn't it the reason we work and prepare? So that we can help those in need?"

"It is not the same," one of the Elders said.

"How is it not?" she asked. "You've known me since birth. Know me well enough to realize I would never, ever bring harm to the people I love and will one day lead."

"But that is exactly what you've done," one of the Elders argued.

Backing away from the semi-circle of men, she turned again, facing the two women in the room. "What's it like to love someone with all your heart? To want to be with them, no matter the cost?"

"Holly, please. Don't say something you regret," her mother whispered.

"Mama, all my life I've wanted God to gift me with a love like yours and Papa's," she said. "And I've *found it*. By *breaking* the rules."

"You've put us in danger," the Elder said, smacking his hand on the table in front of him.

She sent him a chiding glance. "Don't frighten the children, please. There's no need for that."

The Elder's face turned red but he glanced at the little ones and settled back in his seat.

"Rules are needed. I agree," she said quietly, taking the three steps that put her in front of her father. "But I don't think we can ever allow ourselves to be so blinded by rules that we forget our humanity and the love *we claim* for the people of the world. We live as we do because we are dedicated to a greater good. To God's purpose and plan for us to serve. We perform an often thankless job for people who aren't even aware of us other than as cartoon characters. For people who often forget the real reason for Christmas at all. But *we* haven't forgotten—or have we?" she asked, staring at the Elders then turning to face the others present in the room. "We've kept faith in our beliefs and traditions for *hundreds* of years, but because of one mishap—"

"It was quite more than a mishap," the Elder said. "We had to leave the North because of it."

"That's true. But since then we've judged *all* outsiders based on the actions of a few. Where is the mercy and grace and compassion our Heavenly Father expects of us in that? If we go on as we have been, doesn't that mean *we* are the unforgiving?"

She looked at the men in front of her, watched the glances they exchanged. "We lose loved ones and members of our precious community not because of death but because they seek to follow the path God has given *them*—and then we shut the door in their face. We hurt our own by keeping apart families who love each other. To some of us, this is our calling but if one of our own children seeks another path... What may be to them a *greater* path... They're punished for following their calling."

"So you would have us risk everything?" the Elder said.

"I would have us believe," she told him. "We either have faith that God will protect us while we do His will or we don't."

A murmur rose amongst the crowd gathered behind them and a few audible "Amens" could be heard.

"If we believe God controls all things then it stands to reason He *allowed* our North Pole home to be made public for a reason. Maybe we don't know what that reason was but think about the outcome," she said, turning to stare at each Elder for several seconds before moving on to the next. "Had that not happened, we wouldn't have sent our Klaas relatives out into the world to establish new locations. Locations that now serve *more* people. Had the past not happened, the people of the world might not see fit to be as generous and thoughtful to their fellowman during this time, all of which is a celebration of Christ's birth. I don't know the mind of God, but I see an awful lot of good things coming from that single event."

"And we know that all things work together for good to them that love God, to them who are the called according to His purpose," Anna said.

Holly nodded, welcoming the interruption. Her entire body shook and her voice wobbled but she squared her shoulders and took a breath. "All I'm saying is that if we could find a way to interact with our loved ones in the outside world, our people would be happier, perhaps even more productive. Maybe fewer of them would choose to leave if they were able to see their loved ones. After all," Holly turned to Anna, "a mother should be able to see her child and hug grandchildren instead of being punished for dedicating her life to our cause. Why should one have to cost the other?"

Holly tried to gauge the Elders' thoughts despite their stoic expressions.

"And what of you, daughter?" her father said. "Which life would you choose if forced to do so?"

Holly stared at her father for a long moment before turning to the Elders. "Honestly? I don't know."

Her answer created another stir in the crowd, prompting outbursts.

"She is the future. She can't leave."

"She has to stay."

"Why can't they see the world needs us now more than ever?"

Holly listened to the murmurs behind her before turning once more to face the Elders. "I didn't plan this," she told them. "I didn't expect to meet someone from the outside, but I did. And now that I have, now that I've fallen *in love,* how can you expect me to be the person I'm supposed to be if my heart is torn in two? Aren't we battling the worst of the outside world? Why do we do battle amongst ourselves? We're living in fear when God tells us to boldly say, *'The Lord is my helper, and I will not fear what man shall do unto me.'*"

Silence followed her impassioned words and Holly wondered if she'd had any impact. She couldn't tell. The Elders' expressions didn't lend any clues to their thoughts.

"Do you have something to add, Mr. McGarretty?" her father asked, his gaze locked on Ty.

Ty stepped forward but was quickly stopped by the guards.

"No, it's all right," her father said. "Come here. Let us see the man my daughter has brought into our village."

Ty moved toward them with slow steps. "I do have something to say." He held out his hand to her father. "With your permission, sir?"

Holly frowned at the exchange, unsure but willing to bet there was a deeper meaning to Ty's words than the obvious.

"I give it," Nikolas said, shaking Ty's hand.

"Holly's right about us—the outsiders. We're cynical," Ty said to the Elders. "All this time I knew something was going on here and I knew Holly was involved in it, but despite her reassurances that it wasn't illegal or bad, I didn't believe her because of the lies I've been told in the past. Now I understand."

She caught her breath at the look in Ty's yes, his expression. He held out his hands and she didn't hesitate to move toward him, placing her palms in his.

"I'm sorry for not trusting in you."

"I understand," she whispered, her heart pounding hard in her chest.

"But that's not why I fell in love with you."

Love? He was saying it now? Here? "Ty, if it's too soon..."

"It's not. Sweetheart, I fell in love with you the moment I heard your voice on the radio before I crashed. I just didn't know it then."

She couldn't stop the smile forming on her lips and it took every ounce of control she possessed not to throw herself into his arms and kiss him right then. She was overwhelmed with love, joy. The knowledge and awareness of her Creator's actions in her life.

"I promise you I will do whatever it takes to protect you and your home. When I think of the future, I can't imagine not being with you."

Holly stared into Ty's eyes and saw love, sincerity, the strength she needed in a man in the years to come because Ty was humble enough to promise his loyalty in front of her family and members of the Elder Council.

Strong enough to stand up to her. *For* her. "Even if I'm banished to the North Pole?"

"Anywhere you go, I go, too," he said.

"Got that right," George said from behind them. "God's seen fit to call a lot of our family home. I won't let the decision of men separate me from the family I have left."

"In other words," Ty continued, unleashing his intense green gaze on the Elders once more, "if you banish her, you banish us all."

"And me," someone said from the crowd. Mari?

"Me as well," another added.

One by one more and more people called out that they would leave the village and follow Holly wherever she was sent. Hearing it, *seeing* them… Holly couldn't speak, too overwhelmed.

George stood and loudly cleared his throat, drawing everyone's attention.

"You have something to say, Mr. McGarretty?" Nikolas asked.

"Just that it seems a shame to me that people here have to give up something precious," he said, glancing down at Anna. "I know what it's like to lose a wife, a child, and a grandchild to death. I wouldn't wish it on anyone and by banishing people, you're tossing them out when time is precious. I'd think a group like you could find another way to make things work, like Holly said."

"I think we would all like to find a better way but the question is how do we accomplish this? Do you have a suggestion?" her father pressed.

"Actually, I do. We passed a mighty nice fishing lake on the way here. I've never been much of a people person but if my grandson and the kids are leaving Anchorage to live here, I wouldn't mind being close to them. Maybe I could get a piece of that property there and build a house, then if someone wanted to come there and visit one of their relatives that left," he said, glancing down at Anna again, "they could. Wouldn't put the village in danger, then."

Holly stared at George, turned to her father and blinked in surprise. "That's... perfect. It's so simple I can't believe we haven't thought of it before now."

"Not many have left until recent years," her father murmured. "There wasn't a need. The idea holds merit."

"I agree. It would also allow me to be able to support my family," Ty said. "I could land on the lake in the summer and still fly charter when I'm needed."

Ty talked about the future, about what they could do to make things better, just like he was one of them. How could she not be happy about that? "A house there would work for Anna, Papa. And so many of the others. Anyone with family on the outside could arrange a visit so they could see them without bringing their spouses or little ones into the village. It's the perfect compromise for those who are so torn between the two worlds."

Her father nodded his approval before he walked over to the tables where the Elder Council sat. Holly squeezed Ty's hand, so anxious for their verdict she felt ill.

"Say yes," Ty murmured.

She had a hard time tearing her gaze away from the Elders. What were they saying? "Huh? Yes to what?"

"Marriage. Will you marry me, Holly?"

"Yes!" Her announcement drew surprised looks from the Elders but she didn't care. She threw herself into Ty's arms and kissed him, barely aware of her mother and Anna gathering around to congratulate them. George and the children, too.

Finally the sound of her father clearing his voice cut through the happy haze.

"Looks like they've made a decision," Ty told her.

One of the Elders stood. "The Council has decided by unanimous vote that we will overlook the creative scheme brought about by Ms. Klaas on the justification that such an act was necessary to bring an enlightened understanding of how an old law negatively impacts our people."

"No banishment?" Holly asked.

"You will not be banished," her father said. "In fact, in my discussion with the Council I have set my retirement date. I am obviously getting too old for my position if I am unable to see members of my own household hurting due to something I've neglected to change. I think it's time to step down."

Her father's announcement elicited shocked murmurs and comments from the crowd.

"When is this retirement to occur?" Birgit patted Abbie's back when the little girl fussed.

"This year. This is to be my last Christmas. You and I, my dear, will finally be able to take that vacation you've been wanting."

"Papa?" Holly asked. "What I said was not meant to rush you."

"I do not feel rushed, daughter. Quite the opposite. Today you proved yourself to be more than capable of handling the responsibilities and concerns of our people. It's your turn. Yours—and Ty's since you have so emphatically chosen to have him at your side. You and Ty stated your case quite impressively."

Holly laughed, tired from the day, excited by all that had happened and anxious at the news she was about to become the first female Santa in two hundred years.

She glanced up at Ty, her head whirling at all the changes about to take place. So much to do. So much to plan! "What do you say? I'll handle the presents if you fly us. You interested?"

Ty lowered his head and kissed her again. "I thought you'd never ask."

Epilogue

One year later...

Holly was insanely nervous by the big night. Ty had taken to the controls of the sleigh like he was born to them but the closer it came for her to make the deliveries, the happier she was that her husband would be by her side. But before they left for the first part of their trip, she had something else to do—become Santa.

Attendants waited for her nod before they opened the double doors, revealing her to the crowd that waited. Ty stood on the landing with her father and mother, his gaze sweeping her with an expression of love and knowing and excitement of the night to come.

The entire village stood gathered, each holding a candle that twinkled in the twilight. The moment she saw the many faces of her family and friends, her heart pinched. This was her life. Her very own gift from God given to her the moment he knitted her in her mother's womb.

Ty held his hand out for her to take. He looked so handsome, dressed in the special uniform designed just for them to keep out the cold, bitter temperatures. In addition to their suits, they both wore ceremonial mantles that gave Ty a very Batman-ish appearance she found quite attractive.

Ty squeezed her fingers and held her trembling hand firmly in his as he led her to stand before her parents.

"My friends," Nikolas said to the crowd. "It is a special day for us and we look forward to celebrating many, many Christmases in the coming years with Holly as our *Sinterklaas*. So without further ado..."

Her father turned and drew her into his arms, giving her a kiss on each cheek.

"You make us proud, daughter."

"Thank you, Papa."

Birgit stepped forward, a heavily decorated pillow held carefully in her hands. Atop it was the *Sinter Sphere*, a clear glass ball with a cross inside that represented the spirit of Christmas.

Holly inhaled, silently saying a prayer for strength and courage and guidance before she accepted the gift from her father. Once she held it, her father's time worn hands covered hers, warm and reassuring.

"In all ways, may God's work be done."

She repeated the pledge, hot, reverent tears trickling down her cheeks despite her efforts to stay strong.

"Safe travel, my loves," her mother said, first kissing Holly and then Ty.

Her father was next, embracing them both and leading the prayer for the journey.

When the prayer finished, Holly opened her eyes and realized she now stood alone with Ty. Her father and mother had joined the others gathered below the steps, two of the many smiling, beaming faces she loved.

"I love you, Holly McGarretty," Ty said, lowering his head to brush his lips along her jaw. "Or should I say *Santa*?"

"You can call me Red," she said, referring to the nickname Ty had given her when reality had set in after discovering the truth. "Are you ready for this?"

Ty pressed a kiss to her lips, drawing whistles and applause from the crowd before he ended the kiss and held out his arm to escort her down the steps to the waiting sleigh. "Let the night before Christmas begin."

AUTHOR BIO

Kay Lyons Stockham always wanted to be a writer, ever since the age of seven or eight when she copied the pictures out of a Charlie Brown book and rewrote the story because she didn't like the plot. Through the years her stories have changed but one characteristic stayed true—they were all romances. Each and every one of her manuscripts included a love story.

Published in 2005 with Harlequin Enterprises, Kay's first secular romance hit #7 on the bestseller list. Kay has also been a HOLT Medallion, Book Buyers Best and RITA Award nominee with approximately twenty books published in the secular fiction market.

In 2014, Kay lost her beloved father—true hero material—at the age of 85. In the months before and after his death life continued to throw some pretty radical curve balls, leaving Kay struggling to find her creativity and relying heavily on her faith to see her through the valleys.

Reading the Bible brought comfort and in the fall of 2014, Kay rededicated her life to Christ and to becoming a better Christian. Her goals changed and her desire to be a source of light and encouragement to her family, her church, and her readers, stirred the creativity within her to use her God-given talent to spread His word.

To distinguish her secular books from her inspirational novels, Kay took on her maiden name in honor of her father and the inspiration he was as a loving husband of 60 years, a dedicated father, and most importantly, a man of faith.

Look for more inspirational books from Kay Lyons Stockham in the future. For more information regarding her work, please visit Kay's website at www.kaystockham.com and "like" her Kay Stockham Fan Page on Facebook for updates.

20734266R00178

Made in the USA
Middletown, DE
07 June 2015